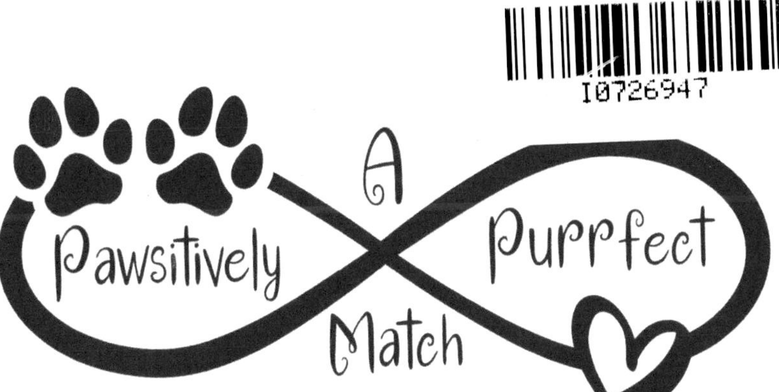
Pawsitively
A
Match
A Purrfect

This Cat's for You

This Cat's for You

PEPPER MCGRAW

Contents

ISBN 978-1-951247-31-7

Edited by J.L. Troughton
PMG Publishing

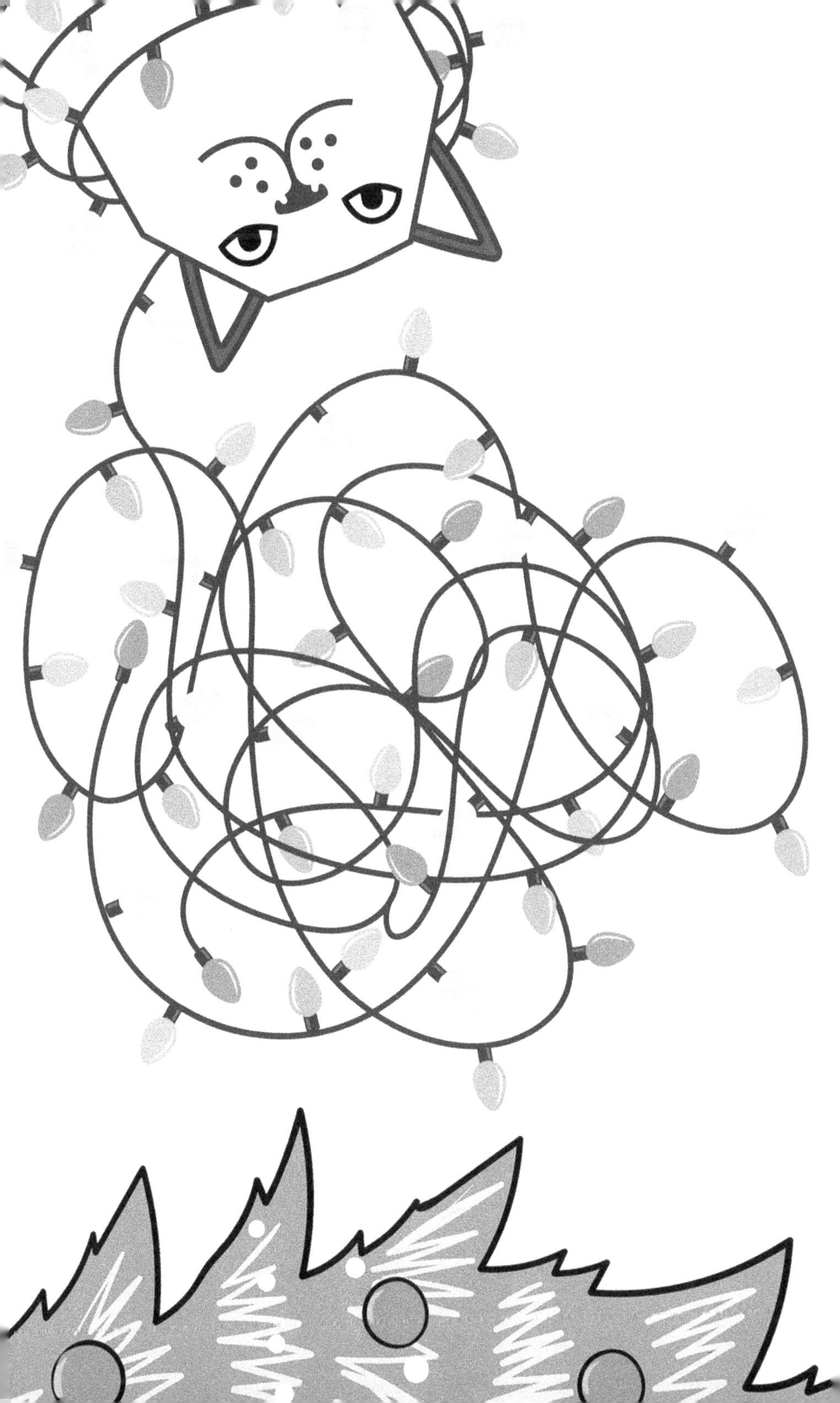

One

BYGUL WAS THE top matchmaker for Pawsitively Purrfect Matches. Being the best wasn't exactly a surprise. He *was* the cat of a goddess, after all, and not just any goddess, but Freyja, herself.

This meant, of course, that he was a very busy cat, with a caseload a mile long. He was often working a number of matches at once or at least setting the wheels in motion for matches down the road.

The goal was always to find the most pawsitively purrfect human companion for each and every cat, which wasn't anywhere near as easy as it sounded.

Matchmaking was highly unpredictable and didn't exactly run on a timeline. After all, some matches just didn't work out as planned and though humans weren't exactly predictable, they were nothing compared to the cats, especially earthbound ones.

Bygul's caseload included homeless cats he came across as he monitored the territories he'd been assigned as well as referrals and other cats brought to his attention by the goddesses. Of course, whenever the goddesses became involved, those cats took priority.

Some matches took longer than others, and once Bygul added matematching to his services, well, they *all* started taking longer than usual.

After all, he liked to see his humans as happy as the cats he matched them with and often this involved finding them not only their purrfect cat companions, but also their purrfect mates.

Unfortunately, that was when things got really complicated.

The other cats at PPM became interested in expanding their services as well and demanded to learn how to make their own mate matches. Thankfully, most cats were fickle at best and they soon lost interest and moved on to other pursuits.

Sadly, there were three cats more stubborn than the rest combined.

This was how Bygul went from working every match on his own to directing a small team made up of three matchmaking cats named Tivali, Soraya and Muezza.

One would think that having a team would make things more efficient, but instead, things just took longer.

He'd tried to explain this to the goddesses, but they seemed to believe that despite the loss of efficiency for him, the other three cats had gained so much with his guidance, that the entire program came out ahead.

He didn't even have the words to describe how much that did not make sense, but there was simply no changing the mind of a goddess.

So for the last year, Bygul had continued in his spot as the top matchmaker at PPM, but he'd done so with three idiots tagging along.

Junior top matchmakers if you will.

They didn't quite deserve the title.

Maybe *junior, junior, junior* top matchmakers, but that would be too much of a mouthful, so Bygul had taken to calling them his junior sidekicks (or idiotic ones depending on his mood).

The point was that because every single match now took longer with a team, the result had been a huge delay in Bygul getting back to Worcester Falls to keep a promise he'd made almost a year ago to an earthbound cat.

At the time, he'd believed Mason Worcester was going to be their final bear match in the Worcester Falls community and Bygul had been thrilled.

Finally.

They could leave the grizzlies behind.

But then at the Christmas cookout at Maggie Winter's place, he'd met an arctic fox.

She'd been sitting on the ground, cuddling a cat in her lap, crooning softly to him while weeping over a bear.

A stupid, idiotic *polar* bear.

Bygul had stretched out beside her, though she couldn't see him, of course, and had laid a paw right on her knee.

Genghis Khat—for of course, it was Maggie's cat she'd been cuddling—had sent him a look, one that had said he needed to fix this and had lifted his head and given her a nudge, making her chuckle and resume her petting.

"It's okay, Genghis Khat," she'd said. "I know not all bears will recognize their mates like Kate did."

Bygul let out a snort.

Kate Worcester hadn't recognized her mate at all!

It had taken a lot of work—days upon days of matematching effort before she and the idiot panther had made their match!

"And I'm just not as bold as Isana." The arctic fox peeked across the yard toward where Isana Meier and her mate, Mason Worcester, were standing arm-in-arm. "She's always been so brave."

More like stubborn and difficult, but whatever.

She sniffed. "It's not like I can just walk up to Wade and —and tell him I'm his mate or—or kiss him or—or anything like that. I bet that's all Isana had to do to win her mate."

Seriously? As if Isana Meier *wanted* Mason Worcester? Didn't she realize it was entirely the other way around?

"Wade and I have known each other our entire lives and he's never looked at me that way. Not even once. And I've always loved him. *Always.*" She let out a huge sigh.

"I don't know why I'm thinking about this again. I accepted long ago that Wade will never be mine. I would

never have the courage to tell him a thing and even if I did
—" She shook her head. "It would be a disaster. So fine. If
he's too stupid to notice what's standing right in front of
him, then that's just fine. Who needs a mate anyway?"

Well, those words were almost like a dare to Bygul's ears.

Unfortunately, his case load just wouldn't wait any
longer.

Not to mention that Tivali, Muezza and Soraya had
their own caseloads and territories.

Unfortunately, this meant the fox would simply have to
wait her turn.

Bygul certainly didn't intend for that turn to take almost
a year to come around. It was just that there were so many
other cases taking priority and unfortunately, none of those
cases were the purrfect match for her.

In the months he'd been busy not helping the arctic fox
make her purrfect matches, he'd managed to do a bit of
sleuthing and had discovered her name was Lumiki and she
was the hostess at The Ice Box in Worcester Falls.

He'd also discovered the Wade she pined for was the bar
manager at the restaurant where she worked.

What was it about these shifter bears?

Clueless, idiotic, stubborn.

Finally, though, everything was coming together.

Things were winding down with most of his cases and it
was time to turn his attention back toward Worcester Falls.

He and his idiotic sidekicks had just managed to deliver
the most purrfect earthbound mother cat and kittens exactly

where they were needed most and were set to launch his most pawsitively purrfect matchmaking plan yet.

Then, because nothing could ever go exactly as planned, the goddesses sprang that crazy cat, Shredder, on them, which unfortunately, pulled their attention away from The Ice Box and things just went sideways from there.

ZACH WAS NOT A HAPPY BEAR.

Most days he really loved his job. He was a kitchen manager at The Ice Box and worked the dinner shift, which allowed him to sleep late.

Unfortunately, today wasn't one of those days.

His older brother Bryce was out for the next two days which meant Zach had to take over some of Bryce's management duties at The Ice Box, including getting up at an ungodly hour to go in and get the restaurant ready to open.

He hated mornings. He hated opening. And he hated the lunch shift.

In other words, today he hated his job.

This was why he parked in the alley and entered The Ice Box from the back.

It was also why he didn't turn on any lights as he headed down the back hallway toward Bryce's office.

It was because he was in a bad mood that he didn't

notice the lights at the front of the restaurant were already on or that the light inside Bryce's office was also on.

It was because he was in such a shitty mood that he din't register the sound of a voice crooning softly from inside Bryce's office until he was halfway through the room.

And it wasn't until he was almost to Bryce's desk that he realized he wasn't alone in that room.

It was only when he saw the epic ass lifted into the air, pointing out from under his brother's desk that he realized he wasn't alone and it was only then that he registered what he was hearing.

"Aren't you the sweetest things I have ever seen? And you are the best mama ever."

Staring at that quivering ass encased in the tightest skirt he had ever seen, Zach felt a wave of heat like he'd never experienced wash over him. Who was this woman and why was she in his brother's office?

"Such a good mama, taking such precious care of your babies. Yes, you are."

There was something familiar about her voice, but he could't quite figure out what it was. Her head was under the desk so he couldn't really see much.

"They're so lucky to have you. Yes, they are. Such sweet babies. Such a good mama."

All Zach could really see was that amazing ass and those incredible, shapely legs and those heels.

No.

The only one he knew around here who wore heels like those was—

It couldn't be.

She wiggled her ass again and another wave of intense heat rolled through him and his polar bear suddenly woke, swiping out with his claws.

Damn. He had to get her out from under that desk before he lost control of his bear.

Zach cleared his throat loudly.

The woman froze for a moment, then slowly wiggled her way out from under the desk.

Zach stared as if in a trance, unable to look away as she slowly, slowly backed out, sank back on her heels and looked up.

Lumiki.

His baby sister, Isana's best friend.

A girl he'd grown up with.

Someone he'd always treated as another little sister, someone he was afraid he'd never see in that same light again.

She was also the hostess for The Ice Box.

"Hi Zach."

"Lumiki." His voice was rough. He cleared his throat, then held out a hand and helped her to her feet. "Ah. What were you doing?"

"Oh! You have a mama cat and kittens." She beamed up at him.

He shook his head. Surely he hadn't heard her right. "What?"

She waved a hand at the desk. "Look! Aren't they adorable?"

He turned and stared.

"Ah, fuck."

Lumiki gasped. "Zach!"

"What? You cannot believe this is a good thing."

"Of course it is! They're adorable and need someone to take care of them."

"Yes. And I know exactly who to call for that."

Lumiki looked devastated at that statement, but he couldn't let that sway him.

Zach had to somehow do all the management crap Bryce usually took care of *plus* his own job today.

He didn't have time to take care of a bunch of kittens.

Besides, this was a restaurant, not a rescue center.

Unlike his sister's place, since she actually ran one of those.

Five minutes later, he couldn't believe his ears. "But I'm your brother! Where's the family loyalty, Isana?" He paced back and forth in front of his brother's desk, trying to ignore Lumiki, who was back under it, cuddling kittens and crooning to their mama, and more importantly, trying to ignore her epic ass.

A practically impossible feat.

"It's because you're my brother that I can, Zachariah. I know good and well that you will take care of that mama and those kittens and ensure they're safe and snug and well-fed through the holidays. Do you know how full my shelter is right now? I'm bursting at the seams! There's just no room, Zach. The mama obviously feels safe in the office right now and that's good enough for me. Just make sure she has enough food and water and the temperature is kept cozy for her. Bring in some blankets so she can snuggle and make a nest for herself and her babies. Get a litter box and just let them be."

Zach groaned. "A litter box?"

"Yes. One with low enough sides the kittens can climb in it. When they're old enough for adoption, I'll help you find homes for them. I promise."

Zach's eyes narrowed. He heard something in her voice that didn't exactly inspire confidence. "Homes that aren't mine, I presume."

Isana let out a tinkling giggle. "Now, Zach, you know I've always said bears would make the worst pet parents."

"You *used* to always say that," he growled darkly. "Then you mated a grizzly who happens to enjoy playing papa bear to a bunch of cats."

"Yes, well, Mason's quite the unique bear. Now, call me if you have questions about how to care for the kittens and good luck. Love you."

"Wait, Isana—"

But it was too late. She'd already hung up.

Zach let out a low growl then dropped his phone on the desk, which prompted a loud hissing sound from beneath it.

"Sorry, sorry." He leaned over the desk to look down at

Lumiki. "Well, you got your wish. Isana can't take them, so we're stuck with them."

"Yay!" Lumiki backed out from under the desk and beamed up at him. "They can be our restaurant kitties!"

"What? Are you crazy? Not a chance. We're finding them homes as soon as they're big enough to be separated from their mom."

Lumiki climbed to her feet and glared at him. "That's not very nice."

"You should be happy I'm letting them stay at all. If Bryce were here, they'd probably already be outside in the alley."

Lumiki raised an eyebrow at him.

"Well, unless someone told Isana." He groaned. "And someone *always* tells Isana."

Lumiki giggled.

Zach narrowed his eyes at her. "And don't think I don't know who's to blame for that! Crazy foxes. Just for that, you're elected for kitten care."

"No way! I will *share* the care with you, but I'm not taking it on all by myself. And just to be clear, I live in an apartment and I see where this is going. There are five kittens plus mama cat under there, so don't even think of trying to get me to adopt all six at the end of this. It's not happening."

Zach barked out a laugh. "Okay. All right. Fine. How about this? We work together and get my cousins to adopt them all."

Lumiki narrowed her eyes at him. "Which cousins? You have like a bazillion."

He grinned. Couldn't argue with the truth. "The bear ones."

She snickered. "You really think you can convince Wade, Steve and Luke to adopt them all?"

"Nope. Doesn't mean it won't be fun trying."

She giggled. "Okay. Let's do it."

"Excellent." Zach thought about it a moment, then grinned. "I think we should make a game of it."

"'What?"

"No. A wager."

"A wager?"

"Yep. Whoever gets the most kittens adopted wins."

Lumiki eyed him suspiciously. "Wins what?"

A ton of truly lascivious, wicked things raced through Zach's mind all at once, but that wasn't why he'd suggested this wager.

Was it?

Oh goddess, maybe it was.

"Zach? What exactly are we wagering?"

"What would you like to wager?" He asked huskily.

She licked her lips, which just gave him all kinds of dirty ideas. "I'm not sure."

"Winner's choice?" He suggested.

She hesitated.

"We've known each other a long time, Lumiki. I would never hurt you. You know that, right?"

"Of course, I know that, Zach."

"So?"

She nodded. "Okay. Winner's choice."

"Shake on it?" He held out his hand.

She slowly slid her hand into his.

They had touched each other a million times over the years.

A casual arm around the shoulders.

A hug.

A kiss on the cheek.

A nudge of the shoulders.

A hip check.

A friendly slap to the back or punch to the arm.

This handshake felt like none of those.

There was something there that he'd never felt before.

Something new.

Something electric.

And he could see by the look in Lumiki's eyes, she felt it too.

It was the start of something new.

Something that might just change their lives forever.

IT WASN'T LONG BEFORE BYGUL REALIZED HE HAD lost control of the entire situation. It was his own fault.

Unfortunately, he'd had to abandon the project with Lumiki at The Ice Box in order to take care of the project with Shredder across town.

The goddesses had insisted and one did not simply say no to Freyja, Ceridwen or Bastet, let alone to all three.

Besides, Bygul quite enjoyed his job as the top matchmaker for Pawsitively Purrfect Matches, thank you very much, and to maintain that honored position, he did have to toe the line every once in a while.

In any case, this meant he sometimes had to delegate and the results weren't always pretty.

So when his brother, Kalyn, a cat responsible for some of the wackiest matches in the history of their organization, asked for the chance to participate in a matematch, Bygul said yes.

It was, of course, a mistake.

He should have just broken up the dream team (extreme sarcasm intended) and sent Muezza or Tivali, or even, goddess forbid, Soraya.

However, those cats were now dedicated to getting Shredder placed with the purrfect human companion and he was reluctant to pull them away from a cause close to their hearts and so, against his better judgment, he'd sent Kalyn.

Of course, he'd given him very specific instructions.

Report back on the romance between the arctic fox, Lumiki, and her polar bear mate, Wade.

And on any bonds forming between them and the earthbound mother cat and her kittens.

Limit all assistance to those situations only.

Bygul had no idea why he thought those instructions would suffice.

After all, no matter the circumstances or the surroundings, at the end of the day, Kalyn was just like the rest of them at PPM—all cat.

KALYN QUITE ENJOYED torturing his pompous brother, Bygul.

In fact, it was the only reason Kalyn had joined his matematching classes the year before.

It had all been for the pleasure of watching his brother's head explode while attempting to wrangle fifty unruly cats into submission.

It had been a ridiculous scenario.

He couldn't believe it when he'd heard the proposal.

Attempting to train *one* cat was like trying to lasso the wind, but fifty cats?

It would be like trying to lasso a tornado in the middle of a hurricane while Mount Vesuvius was erupting.

Literally impossible.

It was quite hilarious watching all those cats drive Bygul quite mad.

Eventually, though, the other cats had all wandered away and the entertainment value had dwindled, so Kalyn had gone off to other pursuits.

It was about time though for him to check back in with Bygul and see what new torture he could rain down on his brother's parade and so he'd started asking around.

It seemed brother Bygul was taking an interest in the polar bears this year.

Plus a mama cat, her kittens and a very dangerous cat named Shredder.

Interesting.

Kalyn was super intrigued by the name Shredder and really wanted to mess with that placement, but then he'd heard the story of that particular cat and decided he'd been through more than enough.

Kalyn was a very bad kitty, it was true, but he wasn't a monster.

And so he'd asked for the mama and kittens instead.

Bygul had been reluctant, of course, but all Kalyn had to do was mention the match that had taken them to the underworld a couple years ago and Bygul had cringed and quickly handed over the match without any complaints at all.

So freaking *hilarious*.

Kalyn loved how easy it was to manipulate Bygul with reminders of that match.

Kalyn truly was a genius.

He'd planned that match down to the very last detail, and in the end, everything had worked out purrfectly.

Perhaps not as purrfectly as Bygul had imagined, but then it wasn't Bygul's match, so that was just fine.

As a bonus, Kalyn got to hold that match over Bygul's head, pretty much into eternity.

The result this time was that Kalyn and Gwyneira, his preferred partner at PPM, would get to spend time at The Ice Box, wreaking havoc on Bygul's latest match between a polar bear named Wade and an arctic fox named Lumiki.

However, within moments of their arrival, Kalyn could see that brother Bygul had everything wrong.

It was the most glorious moment of Kalyn's life.

Because havoc and chaos were things he excelled at, but usually he had to be subtle when causing them so no one realized he was doing it on purpose.

This time, though?

He didn't have to be subtle at all. He could do exactly what brother Bygul asked him to do and gleefully watch the chaos rain down, all in the name of being a helpful, kind, considerate brother.

Wasn't life grand?

Hours later, Lumiki still had no idea what had happened.

She'd spent her entire childhood convinced Wade Meier was her fated mate.

She'd grown up with the Meiers.

All of them.

Isana Meier was her best friend.

Isana always said that even though Bryce and Zach were her brothers and the triplets, Steve, Luke and Wade were her cousins, it was like she'd grown up with five older brothers.

Lumiki always agreed with her because it felt like Isana's older brothers and cousins were hers as well.

Except for Wade.

Wade had been sick when he was a toddler, so he'd started school two years later than Steve and Luke, which meant he was in the same grade as Lumiki and Isana. Even though he was older than them, he never acted like it, which is why he never felt like a brother *or* a cousin.

To Lumiki, Wade was her someday-mate.

The three of them—Isana, Lumiki and Wade—grew up together, running around town, three best friends, getting into trouble together, having fun together, making plans for the future together.

It had seemed inevitable to both Lumiki and Isana that one day Lumiki and Wade would end up together as fated mates.

Except they'd hit the age of majority and nothing had changed.

He'd never looked at her with passion in his eyes and the years had passed without any change in their relationship.

He'd gone to work at his family's restaurant, first as a waiter, then as a bartender, then as the bar manager and Lumiki had done the same, first as a waitress, then later as a hostess, in the hopes that proximity would lead them somewhere, but nothing had ever happened.

Isana spent years trying to talk Lumiki into making a move, especially since bears were notorious for not recognizing their mates when meeting them for the first time—or ever—but that just wasn't Lumiki's style, and so it was up to Wade, and since he was clearly never going to make a move, she'd resigned herself to an empty life without her mate.

This past year, after watching Isana mate with a bear—a grizzly bear, to be sure, but still a bear—Lumiki had started thinking that maybe it was time to consider moving far away, where the pain of seeing her mate every day and not being claimed by him wouldn't be so sharp, but then today had happened.

What the hell did it mean?

She'd crawled out from under Bryce's desk, had looked up at Wade's older cousin, Zach, and there had been a look on his face that had made the fox in her freeze.

A rasp to his voice.

A scent in the room.

But then things had normalized.

A tiny bit.

Then later, the second time she'd been on the floor, she'd looked up at him and his eyes had been full of heat.

And then they'd been staring at each other across the desk.

And he'd proposed that wager.

And there'd been a promise in his eyes that had sent shivers up her spine.

In that moment, she might have done something seriously crazy, but then Isana had swept into the room, demanding to see the kittens.

Zach had immediately launched into another attempt to convince his sister to take the cat and kittens off his hands, but Isana was apparently only there because she didn't trust Zach to go shopping for the cats on his own.

The next thing Lumiki knew, Isana and Zach were off on a mission to "catify The Ice Box," leaving Lumiki alone in the restaurant with Steve on his way to take Zach's place to manage the lunch rush.

Steve.

Who was entirely unqualified to manage a lemonade stand, let alone the lunch rush at The Ice Box.

Even with the help of every arctic fox on staff, he couldn't manage his way out of a paper bag.

The result, of course, was utter chaos.

Lumiki spent the entire day putting out fires left and right, trying to undo the damage Steve left in his wake every ten minutes.

With so much to do and not a lot of time to think, she

was able to hold it together until about fifteen minutes ago when Wade showed up for his shift and headed for the bar.

What happened next—or really, what didn't happen next—was what sent Lumiki reeling.

Her fox didn't even acknowledge Wade's arrival.

Instead, she just kept rolling around in the memory of Zach's scent and the look in his eyes when he proposed that wager.

What in the world was happening right now?

Could she have been wrong all those years?

Was it possible Wade *wasn't* her mate after all?

And if so—she couldn't even comprehend the thought—could it have been *Zach* instead all along?

ZACH WASN'T SURE WHAT WAS GOING ON WITH HIS bear, but he was quite annoyed with Zach. They'd spent hours away from the restaurant already and now that they were back, they'd come in through the alley and hadn't seen Lumiki yet, which was what had set his bear off.

For heaven's sake, you know she's still in the building. We can smell her! We'll see her in a few minutes. I just need to lay down the law with these cats, so settle down!

Thanks to Isana, he'd already wasted so much time today.

A simple errand to grab cat supplies had turned into an hours-long expedition.

He should have known when Isana showed up at the restaurant that she was up to something.

At first, when she'd offered to go with him, he'd been relieved.

Actually, no, at first, he'd tried to convince her to do the shopping without him. But then, he'd decided if she wouldn't go for him, at least having her with him would be helpful since at least she'd know what to buy.

He just hadn't realized knowing what to buy would encompass so damn much.

He should have put his foot down, but frankly, he was afraid of that crazy fox. There was no telling what she would have done if he'd refused to buy half the shit she'd insisted was "necessary."

The end result, of course, was that he'd ended up with a bunch of ridiculous things he didn't need, especially since the cats were only *temporary* guests of the restaurant.

As if spending hours shopping and dragging things into The Ice Box weren't enough, he'd then spent the last hour setting everything up since Isana had abandoned him.

He'd even—he had no idea what had gotten into him—played with the kittens for a while, enticing them out from under the desk with kitten toys he'd somehow ended up buying on that shopping expedition.

Now there were kittens scattered everywhere around the room, chasing balls and toy mice and jumping on cat trees and climbing rope ladders while their mama was napping in a cat bed.

Still under Bryce's desk, of course, because she'd seemed disinclined to follow her kittens out from under her safe spot, so Zach had left her there, but had slid a cat bed under the desk for her.

She hadn't appreciated his efforts, hissing in displeasure, but as soon as he'd walked away, she'd dragged the bed further under the desk, climbed into it and proceeded to circle and knead it with her paws until she'd determined it was satisfactory and had curled up and gone to sleep.

Her purr now filled the office, somehow also filing Zach with a sense of satisfaction.

In fact, the entire office, though cluttered with cat paraphernalia—trees, beds, toys, bowls covered in cat faces, litter boxes with pictures of cats, scratchers and all sorts of things he'd never even known existed—was somehow both ridiculous and satisfying in the extreme.

Zach couldn't even imagine Bryce's reaction when he returned in two days.

He was going to blame Zach for this, but Zach was going to throw Isana under the bus and wouldn't suffer a moment's guilt over it.

It was all her fault, after all.

And Bryce wouldn't even question that fact. They all knew how crazy Isana was.

Zach drew in a deep breath.

Time to get the rules established, then he had to get to work.

He was already so far behind.

And dear goddess, since he'd left Steve in charge, things were probably way worse than if he'd just left no one in charge.

He cringed to think of what Lumiki would have to say to him when he finally emerged from the office.

Lumiki's wrath was nothing to underestimate.

He paced back and forth from one side of the office to the other as he lectured the cats, acutely aware that none of them were paying him any attention.

"Okay, listen. I have to get out there and get to work, but we need to get a few things straight. This room is your domain. You will be safe in here. Out there, well, a lot is happening out there. I cannot guarantee your safety. If you want to explore, there are going to have to be some rules.

"The thing is, we're a shifter establishment in a shifter town and this particular establishment is run by bears. Well, and foxes, but the important part of that statement is the *bears*. Are you hearing me? Because I want to make sure you understand what I'm saying here. There are *bears* out there. We mostly stay in our human forms, but we tend to be a clumsy lot and if we're not paying attention, you could get stepped on. That means you have to pay attention. You have to be faster than a bear. Understand?"

He stopped and looked around the room. Not a one of

the cats were paying him any attention. He sighed. They *were* cats after all.

"Just try to pay attention if you step outside this room. There are other shifters out there as well. Arctic foxes, of course. You won't have to worry about them. But then, there are the customers. Jaguars. Wolves. Bunch of idiots, that lot. But they're not much fans of cats. So keep an eye out. You got me?

"Now, that's all for your safety. Let's talk about restaurant rules. As I mentioned, we're a shifter restaurant, so when we get inspected, it's by shifter organizations and no one really cares about animals on the premises or fur or anything like that, but still, no one wants to find a random strand of fur in their food, so there have to be some rules in place about well, your presence in a restaurant. So listen up.

"All surfaces in the kitchen are off limits to you cats. That's where the food is being prepared. You can hang out on the floor, though, as much as you want, and if any scraps of food fall on the floor, you're welcome to eat them. Now, as for the dining room, where our customers eat—well, shifters don't always mind if animals join them while they're eating. They're not as finicky as humans, but it's always polite to ask. Wait to be invited before jumping up on a table.

"As for the bar, we'll just have to wait and see how it goes. I might set up a section where you can hang out. A cat zone if you will. In fact, now that I think about it, maybe we'll set up a couple tables too. We'll see how that goes too, but for now, only when invited. Understood?"

He stopped pacing again and peeked under the desk at the mama cat.

She opened one eye and gave him a bored look.

He couldn't tell if she'd been paying attention at all.

Honestly, she was a cat.

He was pretty certain she'd understood every word.

Cats were highly intelligent, after all.

Whether she would obey, however, was an entirely different proposition.

It would probably depend on her mood and that would undoubtedly change minute-by-minute, day-by-day.

Great.

Oh, well. At least he'd tried.

"Let me get this straight," Isana said.

They were sitting at the booth furthest from the kitchen where Lumiki could keep an eye on the entire restaurant and see if and when Zach emerged from the back.

Lumiki should be working, but she'd hit panic mode about an hour before and had called Isana in a tizzy, demanding to know when she and Zach would be returning to the restaurant.

Like any good best friend, Isana had immediately wrapped up their shopping excursion and hurried them back to The Ice Box.

She'd left Zach the job of unloading the truck and had hurried inside to find Lumiki, who had immediately dragged her to the back booth and spilled everything.

"So, let me get this straight," Isana said again. "You think *Zach*—my big brother *Zach*, as in the idiot who made dating miserable for both of us in high school and college, who chased off anyone who showed even one iota of interest in either one of us, who showed up on every double date we ever went on to glare at our dates, *that* Zach—might actually, possibly be your *mate*?"

"Yes, that Zach."

Isana burst into laughter. "Well, that explains an awful lot."

"What are you talking about?"

"Come on, think about it. His bear, deep down inside, probably knew even back then that you were his and that's why he stalked our dates."

"Don't be ridiculous. He showed up on your dates too, even when I wasn't there."

"Because he didn't consciously understand what his bear was subconsciously forcing him to do!" Isana exclaimed. "This is wonderful. You know that, right?"

"No," Lumiki said glumly. "It's a total bummer. Zach is so serious. Wade is fun. Wade would have been a blast. Zach is going to drag me down and make me serious too!"

"Or maybe you'll lighten him up, make him have some fun for once," Isana exclaimed. "Also, instead of becoming cousins, you and I'll be sisters, for real!"

Lumiki smiled. "Okay, that *will* be nice, but I just don't get how I could be wrong all those years about Wade. It just doesn't make sense."

"I'm going to ask you a question and I don't want you to get mad."

"Okay."

"Who decided first that Wade was your mate? Was it you or was it your fox?"

"I–honestly, I'm not sure." Lumiki thought about it a moment. "I want to say it was my fox, but I really don't know for sure. It may have been me. I was so grateful that he stood up for me, that he got between me and those bullies that day."

Lumiki nodded. "It makes sense. We were all so young. If your feelings of gratitude got all mixed up and you decided, even subconsciously that he would be the perfect mate—"

"I could have influenced my fox."

"It's possible."

"This is horrible. I've wasted so much time!"

Isana snorted. "Do you think things would have moved any faster if you'd known it was Zach instead of Wade?"

Lumiki groaned. "Probably not. Speaking of Zach, he challenged me to a wager."

"Wow. That was fast. What kind of wager?"

"To see who can get the most kittens adopted first."

"But why? I told him I'd help with that process."

"Why, that sneak."

"I don't get it. What are the stakes of this wager?"

"They felt kind of…" Lumiki's wasn't sure how to describe them.

"Kind of what?"

"Well, he said winner's choice, but it was more the way he said it. And the look on his face."

Isana's eyebrows rose. "Like he was thinking—" She waggled her eyebrows suggestively.

Lumiki groaned and covered her face with her hands. "I don't know. Maybe. Possibly."

Isana grinned. "I like it. But I don't like that you're competing to find the kittens homes." She frowned. "That's just not right."

"Well, he was going to start with the triplets."

Isana gasped. "Are you serious right now?"

Lumiki nodded.

"I'm not approving Steve under any circumstances, so you call me if he agrees. But the other two, maybe. You know how I feel about giving pets as gifts though. If Zach tries to give the kittens to anyone, you call me. And no coercing anyone to adopt those kittens. They need to go to good homes."

"Of course."

Three

"FINALLY!" GWYNEIRA EXCLAIMED. "I thought that polar was never going to arrive!"

Kalyn grinned.

Gwyneira was so hilariously impatient. It was one of the reasons they worked so well together.

That and the fact they both found Bygul to be impossibly arrogant and pompous and thoroughly enjoyed torturing him.

In fact, it was one of their favorite pastimes.

It was Kalyn's, simply because he had the misfortune of being Bygul's younger brother, and Gwyneira's because she'd had a run-in with Bygul on a match years before and had never forgiven him for the encounter.

Kalyn had no idea what had happened and she wasn't sharing, but apparently Bygul had been rude and arrogant and condescending—witness Kalyn's lack of surprise—and

Gwyneira had dedicated herself to making Bygul's life a misery ever since.

Now that Wade Meier had finally arrived, the fun could finally begin.

"It's not like we're breaking any rules." Gwyneira stretched slowly.

"Of course not." Kalyn climbed to his feet. "After all, Bygul did tell us Wade Meier is Lumiki's mate."

"Bygul does like to share that he's rarely wrong on these matters."

"A very good point. We'll need to help that mating along as best as we can."

"It would be what any good representative of Pawsitively Purrfect Matches would do," Gwyneira said.

"Agreed. I"ll take care of the fox."

"And I'll herd the bear."

FROM WHERE LUMIKI AND ISANA WHERE SITTING, they were in the perfect position to observe everything that went on in the restaurant—the good, the bad and the ugly.

Lumiki could see when a problem began, when it was headed off at the pass, when it rose to crisis level, when that crisis was averted and when it escalated to a full-on emergency.

She also saw when Steve waded in and made things worse and when Wade came to the rescue and smoothed things over.

"Can you believe they're brothers?" she asked Isana.

Isana rolled her eyes. "What's more unbelievable is that Steve, Luke and Wade are triplets."

So true.

Steve was so emotional and useless.

Luke was so calm and rational.

And Wade? Wade was just fun.

Truthfully, it was hard to remember they were triplets at all.

They were all so different.

Steve and Luke were like two sides of one coin and while Lumiki adored them both, there was only one she would wish to be stranded on a desert island with because only one had innate survival skills. The other would be dead weight.

Of course, they were both still assholes.

In entirely different ways.

But if she really had a choice, she'd choose Wade every time because with Wade, she'd not only survive the experience, but she'd also thrive.

"I should get back to work. Poor Wade keeps having to step in when he really needs to be getting the bar ready to open."

"Eh. You realize you've been the acting front of house manager for years and they're still only paying you like you're a hostess."

Lumiki rolled her eyes. "Ah, but I don't have the title. With the title comes added responsibility."

"But you take it on anyway."

"And I can choose not to at any time. Like right now when I'm ignoring all the crises going on around us."

Isana laughed. "Okay. Fair point."

"I should get back to work though."

"Yeah, and I should get back to the center. Sarah could probably use my help."

Lumiki and Isana left the booth and walked toward the front entrance.

They paused next to the hostess stand, exchanged hugs and promised to catch up later in the week.

Isana headed out the door and Lumiki turned, reaching for her reservation book.

The heel on her left shoe chose that moment to snap.

She let out a cry and grabbed for the stand, but missed.

She closed her eyes in anticipation of slamming to the unforgiving marble floors, but instead was caught at the last moment in someone's arms.

"Are you okay?"

She opened her eyes and found herself braced against Wade's chest, staring into his eyes.

He helped steady her on her feet, keeping his hands on her waist as she wobbled a little on her uneven heels.

Wow.

Just the day before—no, even six *hours* before—she

would have been thrilled to be caught in his arms, but now, her fox didn't even blink an eye.

Even more disconcerting, she couldn't help but wish it had been *Zach* who had saved her.

"Um, yes. Thanks, Wade." She set a hand on the hostess stand to her right and was about to step out of her heels when a bear's enraged roar reverberated through the restaurant and Wade was suddenly ripped away, causing her to wobble on her heels again.

Thank goodness she was holding onto the hostess stand this time.

She stared in amazement as Zach launched his cousin across the lobby of the restaurant, sending customers scrambling out of the way.

With another enraged roar, Zach stamped forward, fists clenched, clearly not yet finished with his cousin.

Lumiki kicked off her heels and raced after Zach, skidding in front of him and slamming the palms of her hands against his chest. "Zach! Stop it! The heel on my shoe snapped and Wade saved me from a nasty fall."

Zach glared down at her. His polar bear had taken over his eyes, so that every bit of the whites had been overtaken by a brown so dark they seemed almost black. "He doesn't get to touch you." His voice was the deep growl of his bear.

"He was just trying to help me." Lumiki flung a look over her shoulder at Wade, worried he'd been hurt.

Wade grinned at her, climbed to his feet and dusted

himself off. "So that's the way of it, is it? Took your bear long enough to figure things out, don't you think?"

"What are you talking about?" Zach rumbled.

"Oh, nothing." Wade chuckled. "This is going to be fun. I'd give you a hug, Lumiki, but I don't think Zach's bear would like that. Just know that I approve. I'll be getting back to work now. Have fun." He gave them a wide berth and sauntered back into the main part of the restaurant, headed for the bar.

Lumiki faced Zach and scowled at him. "What the heck was that? Wade's your cousin and we've been best friends our whole lives! You've never had a problem with us touching before."

He scowled at her. "Well, clearly my bear's lost his mind so for everyone's sake, try not to rile him up, okay?"

"If you say so."

He grunted, then stamped off.

Lumiki shook her head. "Everyone's gone mad around here." She headed for the hostess stand, scooping up her heels along the way. She glanced around at the shifters waiting to be seated. "All right. Who's next?"

Gwyneira licked a paw and rubbed her head with it . "You just had to ruin her shoe, didn't you?"

"It was effective, wasn't it?" Kalyn demanded.

"Effective yes, but you do realize humans consider high heels to be tools of romantic persuasion, right?"

"That makes no sense whatsoever."

"Well, they *are* humans."

"Which makes them thoroughly predictable." Kalyn grinned at the memory of the polar bear's roar the moment he caught sight of the fox in his cousin's arms.

For a moment there, he'd thought his talents for chaos had reached new heights and they were about to witness a true bear brawl, but then the arctic fox had interfered.

Ah, well.

Maybe next time.

ZACH'S BEAR WAS FURIOUS. HE KEPT DEMANDING that Zach kill Wade.

He's our cousin for goddess' sake. We can't kill our cousin! Aunt Lucy would never forgive us.

His bear just grumbled irritably.

Zach knew it was weird that he and his bear had entire conversations. He didn't know a single other bear who did the same.

Or any other shifter for that matter.

But he'd been aware of his bear communicating with

him for as long as he remembered. First in pictures, then in grumbled words and phrases and later in short sentences.

His brother and cousins teased him good-naturedly about hearing voices, but Zach knew they were a little envious of his relationship with his bear. It was definitely unique.

And also a pain in the ass sometimes.

He had definite opinions that weren't always in line with Zach's opinions.

Although at the moment, Zach happened to be in agreement.

Wade needed to keep his hands to himself.

Zach just preferred not to think about why he felt this way so strongly when he'd never been bothered by Wade's touchy-feely tendencies before.

Zach spent the rest of his shift avoiding both Lumiki and Wade, but also plotting his revenge.

It had only taken a few moments inside the office for inspiration to strike.

The bar had always been Wade's domain.

Now that Zach had time to contemplate it, though, he believed what Wade needed was a bar kitty. Maybe even two. Or three. Or perhaps five would be the perfect number.

Yep.

Five bar kitties coming right up.

By the end of her shift, Lumiki was feeling completely let down.

Zach had avoided her the entire rest of her shift, which mean they hadn't discussed the wager or anything.

Maybe he'd forgotten about it or changed his mind.

When her shift was over, she even lingered in the back office, checking out the new setup and playing with the kittens, hoping he'd stop by so they could discuss the plan, but he never did.

So she'd finally gone home alone to sulk.

Of course, Isana called for an update and had been just as annoyed as Lumiki to hear there *were* no updates.

"Nothing?" Isana exclaimed incredulously.

"Nothing," Lumiki said morosely. "Well, unless you count when he threw Wade across the lobby."

"That totally counts. Tell me everything!"

So Lumiki told her about the lobby encounter, but ended with how Zach stamped away and didn't speak a word to her for the remainder of her shift.

"What is *wrong* with that brother of mine?" Isana demanded.

"He's a bear," Lumiki said.

"Hey now!" Mason, Isana's mate, hollered in the background. "I resemble that!"

Lumiki giggled.

"Well, just be patient," Isana said. "In their plodding, lumbering way, bears do usually figure things out."

A loud growling sound filled the air.

Isana giggled. "Gotta go, Lumiki."

Lumiki rolled her eyes. "Fine. Go have fun with your bear-mate. I'll just sit here, pining away for my maybe-one."

"Oh, I think he's your definite-mate based on his reaction to Wade holding you in his arms. It's just taking a bit of time for him and his bear to face reality."

"Hm. Well, they'd better get with the program fast because I'm running out of patience."

LUMIKI HAD NO IDEA WHAT SHE EXPECTED WHEN she walked into The Ice Box the next day, but it definitely wasn't what she found.

"What do you think?"

Lumiki jumped and glanced over her shoulder. "Oh, Zach. You startled me. Wade's going to kill you." She gestured toward the bar, where a neon sign now declared it to be the "Cat Zone."

"Are you really going to let the cats wander the bar?"

He shrugged. "If they want to."

"They're cats. They're going to want to wander everywhere."

He grinned. "Of course, they will, but it's going to annoy Wade to have a sign that makes it seem like we've given them permission to wander over there."

Lumiki giggled. "You're so evil."

"It's my best quality, don't you think? Listen, about the wager. I'm thinking we should just try and get Wade to adopt them all."

"Are you serious? All five kittens?"

"Yep."

"He'll never go for it."

"Never say never. So that's today's challenge. Whoever convinces Wade to adopt more kittens wins."

Lumiki shook her head. "That doesn't even make sense. He probably won't adopt any."

"Then neither one of us will win."

She rolled her eyes. "Fine. But Isana gets final approval on all adoptions."

Zach scowled. "Do you know what a hardass she is? We'll be lucky to get any kittens adopted if she has to approve every one."

"Sorry. Those are the rules. She gave me a stack of applications and said anyone interested has to fill one out."

Zach left out a huff of exasperation. "She got to you, didn't she? She's such a pain in the ass. Fine. She gets final say, but don't say I didn't warn you if at the end of all this, you end up with five kittens snuggled in your bed with you."

Lumiki scowled at the look on his face. "Don't even put that out there because it's not happening."

"Right. Well, good luck to you. Wade won't be in until three, so you have until then to figure out your strategy. May the best shifter win."

THE LUNCH RUSH WAS ALMOST OVER WHEN WADE finally arrived. He took one look at the bar area and roared Zach's name.

The customers still lingering in the restaurant all laughed at his reaction.

There had been much speculation throughout the day about what Wade's reaction would be.

Some predicted he would be intrigued, others that he would be angry and still others that he would be pleased. Most thought he would be angry, of course, and they were right.

Zach came striding through the restaurant at that moment, two tabby kittens in his arms. "Why, hello, Wade, cousin mine. Happy to see you this afternoon." He headed for the bar. "Have you noticed the wonderful additions we've made to the bar?"

He pressed a button on the wall and two panels on the bar retreated, revealing the inside cabinets had been transformed into tiny kitty retreats, with walls made of sisal rope for scratching and the floors transformed into kitty beds.

"Of course, these cat cabinets aren't complete without their own kittens, so my dear cousin Wade, these cats are for you." With that, Zach plopped the two tabbies on top of the bar and stepped back.

Wade glared at him over the bar. "Are you being serious right now? You can't just give me two kittens."

"Of course I can," Zach said cheerfully.

Lumiki groaned softly, pulled out her phone and called Isana. "The insanity has already begun."

Isana chuckled. "What on earth are you talking about?"

"Zach just gifted two kittens to Wade."

"I'm on my way."

"Total dirty pool, Lumiki." Zach glared at Lumiki after dragging her into the office. He couldn't *believe* she'd called his sister.

"All's fair in love and war." Lumiki shrugged. "And giving away two kittens isn't the same as getting them adopted, as you very well know."

"Nine-tenths is some sort of possession in the eyes of the law. Or something like that."

Lumiki giggled. "It doesn't work like that and you know

it. Now I have to get back to work." She whirled toward the door, but Zach caught her hand and pulled her back, tugging her into his arms.

"I think you owe me a forfeit," he murmured against her lips. "I'm pretty sure you broke the rules of our wager."

"Me?" Lumiki exclaimed. "I'm the not the one who—"

He captured her lips with his and whatever she was going to say was lost in the heat of the moment.

Her lips were so incredibly soft, and his bear, who had been restless and agitated all morning long, went still, then lunged forward, wrapping itself in her scent and taste.

It took every bit of Zach's strength of will to wrestle the bear back and to end the kiss gently. "Winner's choice just got a whole lot more interesting," he murmured against her lips before setting her aside and striding from the office.

Four

"UGH," KALYN EXCLAIMED. "The polar finally made a move."

"I know," Gwyneira said. "It's annoying. Bears can go years plodding along without ever realizing their mate is right by their side and then suddenly—warp speed."

"At exactly the wrong time," Kalyn agreed.

Kalyn and Gwyneira both let out yowls of startlement when Bygul suddenly popped into the room beside them.

Kalyn launched himself at Bygul and the two rolled around on the floor wrestling until Gwyneira swatted them both and snapped, "Stop acting like a couple of kittens and get serious. Bygul, why are you here?"

The two cats took one last swipe at each other before stretching and sitting up straight.

"Just checking in," Bygul said. "Wanted to see how the

matches are coming along. Have Wade and Lumiki fallen in love yet?"

"Not even close," Kalyn said.

Bygul let out a growl of disappointment. "Well, why not? You've been here two days already. Are they at least bonding with the cats?" He glanced into the restaurant and saw Wade was petting one tabby kitten on the bar while another played nearby. "Well, that's all right then. What about Lumiki?"

"She definitely likes all of the cats," Gwyneira said.

"But there are some stumbling blocks with the mating," Kalyn said.

"What kind of stumbling blocks?" Bygul demanded.

"Wade doesn't seem that interested in her," Gwyneira said.

Nor did Lumiki seem that interested in him anymore, but Kalyn didn't think Bygul needed to know that at the moment.

"*Bears.*" Bygul shook his head. "So stubborn. Well, just keep working on it. See what you can do about getting Lumiki to spend as much time as possible at the bar. Surely if she's in Wade's presence enough, the polar will come to his senses and realize she's his mate."

"We'll do our best," Gwyneira said cheerfully.

"Right. I've gotta get back to Shredder. That cat is something else. Let me know if you two need anything." With that, Bygul was gone.

"What do you think about recruiting the earthbound cats to help with the mischief-making?" Kalyn asked.

Gwyneira let out a rumble of agreement. "I think that sounds like a lot fun."

Lumiki stared after Zach, fingers on her lips, then sank down onto the floor. "Unbelievable," she whispered. "What are we doing?"

The mama cat wandered over and climbed onto her lap.

"Hey, baby." She started petting the cat.

A few moments later, three other kittens were climbing all over her as well.

They were all so adorable, she spent the next twenty minutes hiding out in the office and playing with cats.

Eventually, though, she realized she really couldn't hide out much longer.

"I suppose I should get back out on the floor. Love you, darlings. We really do need to come up with some names for you guys. I'll be thinking about it." She handed out hugs and kisses, then rose to her feet and headed for the door.

She wasn't exactly paying attention, which is how when she opened the door, the mama cat and all three kittens managed to barrel past her before she even got one foot over the threshold.

"Hey! Wait!"

Crap.

She left the door open and hurried after the cats who all raced straight down the hallway, past the kitchen and into the restaurant itself.

It was as if they knew exactly where they were going as they weaved in and out of tables through the restaurant to the other side, making a beeline for the bar and where the other two kittens were.

Maybe they were just following the scent trail of their siblings, although Zach had carried them across the restaurant so she didn't know how that was possible.

Somehow, though she was hurrying as fast as she could, the cats still all beat her to the bar.

The mama cat made her way behind the bar, where she wrapped herself around Wade's feet.

Wade looked down at her, a surprised look on his face. "Well, hello there, darlin'."

"Sorry about that, Wade," Lumiki said, arriving at his side, a bit breathless. "They all got away from me."

"All?"

At that moment, a black kitten launched itself onto the bar and skidded straight across it.

Wade reached out and scooped it into his hands, cuddling it close. "Well, what are you up to?" He set it back onto the floor. "Exactly how many kittens are there wandering around this place?"

"Five and mama there."

"Where'd they come from?"

Lumiki shrugged. "They just showed up the other day and we've been feeding them until we can find them good homes. I was kind of hoping Bryce and Zach would agree to letting them become Ice Box mascots, but I don't think Zach's in favor of that idea."

Wade grinned. "Well, Zach did put that sign up there."

"Pretty sure that was a joke. I think he's hoping you'll adopt all the cats and take them home with you. Will you?"

Wade laughed. "I do think they're adorable, but not a chance in hell."

Lumiki giggled. "That's what I figured. I'll tell Zach you said no."

At that moment a bear's roar came from the other side of the restaurant.

Lumiki sighed. "Now what?"

A quick glance showed them Zach stamping toward them, a thunderous look on his face.

Wade chuckled. "You should probably back away, Lumiki."

"Huh?"

"You're standing a little close."

"Oh, for heaven's sake." Lumiki scowled, spun and stalked around the bar. She held up her hand and snapped, "Don't even start," when Zach opened his mouth to begin what she was sure was going to be a very loud yelling lecture.

"In case you were wondering, Wade said no."

Zach looked confused.

"I brought the mama cat and the other three kittens over to introduce him. He said no to adopting any of them, so that's a no on taking them home to his place. However, he might be open to keeping them here at The Ice Box as mascots for his bar."

Wade made a choking sound behind her, but didn't contradict her so Lumiki counted that as a win.

Zach glared at her. "*That* is not an option."

"Then I guess we're still trying to find families for the kittens."

"Steve was going to be my next target."

"Look, you know I love Steve, but he's unreliable at best. He's temperamental and I'm not sure he can be trusted to care for himself, let alone a bunch of kittens."

"Eh, he's not that bad."

ZACH SHOULD PROBABLY FEEL BAD FOR THE LIE HE just told because honestly?

Steve really *was* that bad.

However, Zach wasn't too concerned about it because there was no way Steve would *ever* consent to adopting one kitten, let alone five.

Steve was the most self-centered polar bear Zach had

ever met and frankly, that was saying a lot since polars could be a bit self-involved.

Zach had always enjoyed teasing Lumiki, but now he found himself obsessed with her every reaction—each tiny expression on her face, the crinkle of her nose, the light in her eyes.

Basically, Zach—and his bear—were enchanted.

"Not that bad?" Lumiki exclaimed. "Zach, he forgot to feed the goldfish he adopted last year!"

Zach made a face. That had been a disaster. No one could figure out why Steve had even decided to adopt a goldfish. It made no sense. And Steve refused to talk about it.

"Right. Well, if he agrees—which he probably won't—but if he does, we'll all check in on him and make sure he doesn't forget. Right?"

"Fine, but I want it stated for the record that this is terrible idea and let's not forget—Isana gets final say. Where is she anyway?"

"She delivered her lecture and left." Zach glared at Lumiki. "I still can't believe you called her."

Lumiki shrugged. "She made me promise. No gifting cats."

He rolled his eyes. "Whatever. Let's go chat with Steve." He grabbed her hand and dragged her toward the kitchen.

"Hey! Aren't you going to take the kittens with you?" Wade called after them.

Zach just waved a hand at him. "They're cats. They'll go

where they want to go and they'll stay where they want to stay."

Lumiki giggled. "You're terrible."

"But I'm not wrong, am I?"

A few minutes later, they walked into the kitchen, threaded their way through the various sections toward the back. They left the heat of the kitchen and entered the cooler pastry kitchen where Steve worked as a pastry chef.

The man's talent with desserts was truly unparalleled and was probably the only reason he'd survived to adulthood.

"Hi, Steve." Lumiki bounced over to his side, where he was slowly, methodically placing berries on top of some fancy looking chocolate mousse concoction.

He ignored her.

"So we were wondering. We have five adorable kittens who really need a loving home and we were wondering if you would like to adopt them. We think you'd make a wonderful kitty papa."

All around them, the hustle and bustle of chefs coming in and out to pick up pastries to deliver to the pass died down, and as word spread to the outer kitchen of Lumiki's question, conversation and movement died down there as well as everyone strained to hear Steve's response, which was of course, nothing at all.

"Steve?"

Silence.

Zach and Lumiki watched as Steve carefully finished

placing the final berry on his pastry creation and straightened to a standing position. He stepped back and nodded. "Mark!"

The assistant pastry chef raced forward. "Yes, Steve."

"Take this to the pass at once."

"Yes, Steve."

"And be careful with it. It's delicate. Those berries shouldn't shift even one millimeter in transit."

"Of course, Steve."

The three of them watched as Mark carefully lifted the white bowl as if it were a bomb that might explode at any moment, then shuffled toward the door in that same frozen position, bowl cupped between his hands, arms frozen in position, his entire torso somehow not moving as his legs shuffled him along out the door.

Zach nudged Lumiki in the side as soon as Mark made it through the door and was out of sight. "Breathe," he muttered.

She let out a whoosh of air. "That was intense."

Steve whirled to face them. "What do you want?"

"Kittens!" Lumiki exclaimed. "We have five. Would you like to adopt them?"

"No. Go away."

"Okay. See you later." Lumiki practically skipped out.

Zach just shook his head, chuckled and followed her.

"I can't believe you offered that psycho five kittens!" Carol, one of the kitchen workers, stepped into Lumiki's path and glared at her.

"Hey, take it up with Zach." Lumiki pointed her thumb over her shoulder at Zach. "It was his idea. I told him it was a terrible idea, but he insisted."

Carol set her hands on her hips and glared at him. "You should know better, Zach!"

Zach grinned. "I knew he'd say no. Besides, I'm just covering my bases, so when Isana wants me to take the cats, I can legitimately say that I've tried to find other people and haven't succeeded, so now it's her turn to try and find homes for them. Hey, you wouldn't happen to be in the market for some kittens, would you?"

Carol growled at him. "Do I look like a sucker to you? Not a chance, mister." She turned back to her station and got to work.

Zach let out a growl. "See, Lumiki? I had it right all along."

"What are you talking about?"

"You don't find homes for kittens by *asking* people."

"Whatever. So Luke next?"

"Luke's not in until next week. Maybe we can get a customer to adopt a kitten or two. For now, though, our shift's over." He caught her hand in his and pulled her out of the kitchen and down the hall toward the office. "So, since Day 1 is officially behind us, I'm claiming today's winnings."

"What winnings? We haven't gotten a single cat adopted."

"Exactly. Which means we both lost, which also means

we both won, so I guess that means we both get to choose our winnings. I choose a date. With you. Tonight."

Lumiki smiled. "Really?"

"Yes. Really. I'll pick you up at your house. Seven o'clock work?"

"Yes!"

Lumiki called Isana on her way home, barely able to contain her excitement.

It felt slightly strange to be calling Isana to talk about going on her first date with Zach, not Wade, but they'd both made the leap with surprising ease. Though they'd spent years speaking of Lumiki's future with Wade, it hadn't taken long for them to make the switch and now every conversation centered around Zach.

"What are you going to wear?" Isana asked.

"I don't know!" Lumiki wailed.

"The blue dress," Isana said. "It brings out your eyes."

And that quickly, the crisis was over.

They spent the rest of the ride speculating about where he would take her. After all, the best restaurant in town was owned by his family, so there was no way he would be taking her there.

"He'll probably just take me to another Shenanigans

restaurant," Lumiki said. "It would make the most sense and would be the safest choice."

"I suppose. There really aren't a lot of choices around, unless you want to go to a human establishment or the Greensboro Diner."

Lumiki giggled. "That'd be okay, I guess. It's been a long time since we went there. It'd be like a blast from the past, revisiting our high school days."

Isana snickered. "Yeah, but Zach wasn't in high school when we were in high school."

"True, but he did stalk our dates there."

They both burst into laughter.

"Oh, my gosh, if he takes you to the diner, you have to text me a selfie and tell me all about it."

"Now I'm really hoping he does."

Lumiki was still chuckling over their conversation when she opened the door to Zach's knock a couple hours later.

Zach's eyes lit up when he saw her. "Lumiki," he murmured. "You are exquisite." He leaned forward and captured her lips in a searing kiss that sent a wave of heat down Lumiki's spine.

He pulled away. "You ready?"

She nodded, filled with anticipation and hope.

Once they were on their way, he said, "I really wasn't sure what to do for this first date. I could take you to a different Shenanigans, but we'll probably run into people we know and it could get annoying fast. I also thought about packing us a picnic dinner from the Ice Box, which we will definitely have to do at some point, but then it occurred to me that really what I owe you is a slew of first dates."

Lumiki shook her head. "I—I don't know what you mean."

"You'll see."

He drove them out of Worcester Falls and to Lumiki's shock, headed into Pleasantville, a human town, where he pulled into, of all places, the parking lot of a human restaurant chain.

"Chili's?"

He grinned at her. "Do you remember the last time you were here?'

Just like that, memories flooded her.

Her very first solo, non-double date at seventeen had been with a human boy named Jeremy Stein. He'd been eighteen years old and super cute. Every girl in her grade had wanted to date him and he'd asked *her*.

Jeremy had picked her up in his daddy's pickup truck and she'd been mortified when they'd arrived in this very parking lot to discover Zach leaning against *his* truck, glaring at them as they'd entered the restaurant.

Zach had somehow managed to get the booth right across from them and had spent the entire dinner glaring at poor Jeremy, who hadn't dared to even touch her all night long.

She'd never gotten another date with Jeremy again.

Or any other boy that year.

Lumiki glared at Zach.

"Do you really think reminding me of that fiasco is the right way to go for our first date, Zachariah Meier?"

He grinned at her. "Just hoping to make up for my past misdeeds, Ms. Aleia."

She rolled her eyes, but couldn't quite hide her smile.

Of course, as they went inside, she insisted on taking a selfie of the two of them at the front entrance and sending it to Isana, who immediately replied with a series of laughing emojis. She then took a couple selfies of the two of them in their booth and of their food.

They spent hours talking and reminiscing about dates gone wrong and wondering how they could have missed what was in front of them for so very long.

They drove back to Worcester Falls holding hands and Zach walked her to her front door.

Lumiki turned to face him, heart pounding and weak in the knees. "Would you like to come in?"

"Ah, Lumiki. If I come in, I won't want to leave."

She smiled at him. "I'm okay with that."

He leaned forward, wrapped an arm around her waist and pulled her close, hugging her tight. He buried his face in her neck and murmured in her ear, "I want that more than you can know, I truly do. You mean more to me than just one night, Lumiki mine. My bear thinks you are its mate."

Lumiki gasped and her heart leapt in joy.

Zach pulled back and stared at her.

She nodded. "I think my fox believes that as well."

"Yes. And so I want to take this as slow as we need to. I

want to make sure when we do this, we do it right, so that when we take that final step— " He leaned forward and caught her lips with his in a searing kiss that sent waves of heat traveling from every single point in her body, from her core outward, so that she could barely breathe through the conflagration.

He pulled back again. "—we will know, my love, that it is forever."

Five

"WE'RE DOOMED," KALYN said. "Not even the earthbound cats can save the romance now."

Gwyneira stretched lazily. "Were we trying to save a romance? Or were we just muddying the waters and you know, making life difficult for Bygul?"

Kalyn twitched an ear. "Good point. Then I suppose I should say we've failed to muddy the waters. They're looking pretty clear at the moment."

"Right. Then perhaps we should recruit some additional helpers." Gwyneira slowly paced from side of the room to the other. "The oldest brother should show up tomorrow and he's going to be quite surprised to find cats all over the restaurant. We can probably use that to our advantage."

"Oooh. And it's holiday party season, so—"

"Christmas trees and mistletoe!"

Zach decided he was an idiot. There was no other word for it.

He'd had the opportunity to claim Lumiki, to spend the night in her bed, with her in his arms, and instead, he'd kissed her and sent her off into her apartment alone.

He'd then gone home alone himself.

For some idiotic reason he couldn't even justify in the light of day.

Because he'd wanted it to be right, to ensure they would be together forever.

Which was ridiculous since he was pretty sure if he'd gone ahead and claimed her the night before, their forever would have started right then since there was no way he'd have let her go afterwards.

Instead, though, he'd been an idiot and sent her off to bed alone.

So, here he was the next day, still unmated, plus tired and cranky to boot.

To make matters worse, he'd just remembered that Bryce was scheduled to return to work this morning and he was sure to hear about the cats who had taken over his office (and the bar) as well as all the work Zach hadn't gotten done in his absence because, well, Zach had been distracted.

By his mate.

Lumiki.

He just couldn't believe that she'd been right there all these years and he'd never known who she was to him.

Of course, remembering how angry he used to get every time Lumiki went on a date, he had to wonder whether deep down inside, his bear had always known.

Not that he could ask his bear since, despite having always been rather talkative with Zach, his bear had been surprisingly quiet on the subject.

In fact, if Zach didn't know any better, he'd think his bear was sulking.

With all of this on his mind, it was no wonder Zach arrived at The Ice Box that morning with a cranky attitude and zero desire to work.

He was the first to arrive at the restaurant and entered from the back alley.

He made his way down the hallway in the dark, turned into the office, flipped on the light and startled cats who were climbing trees, chasing balls and napping all over the room.

He grinned and headed across to the desk chair where he settled and peeked under the desk at the mama cat.

She let out a tiny hiss and he responded by dangling a wand toy in front of her. She batted at it and he played with her with one hand while checking a few inventory spreadsheets with the other.

A couple kittens stopped by for a visit and he absentmindedly gave them a few pats on the head, tossed a few balls for them to chase and cuddled one to his chest.

He checked a few more things, then scratched mama's head, put the wand toy away, pat a few more kittens and tried to ignore the couch that was calling his name on the way out.

Lumiki let herself into The Ice Box, switching on lights as she went.

This was so weird.

Bryce was supposed to be back today and he would usually be here by now.

Zach usually worked a later shift, but he was planning to come in early as well because everyone was anticipating Bryce freaking out about the cats.

However, the place was still dark and silent. Usually there would be music playing and Zach would either be at the bar or in the office working.

She set her purse down at the hostess stand and walked down the hallway toward the back office. She'd just reached the door when it suddenly opened and a dark shadow stepped out.

She jerked back with a startled scream that she cut off when she realized who it was. "Damnit, Zach. You scared me to death!" She clutched her chest, trying to catch her breath.

"Hey, Lumiki. Thought you'd know it was me."

"None of the lights were on. I didn't think anyone else was here!" She should have recognized his scent, but damn. She really had thought no one was in the building.

"Oh, yeah, sorry. I parked in the alley." He grinned at her. "Glad you're here though." He hooked an arm around her waist and dragged her into the office with him, slamming the door closed behind them.

"What are you doing?"

"Well." He walked backwards, pulling her with him, until the back of his legs hit the couch. He glanced over his shoulder, then fell backwards, pulling her down on top of him.

The feel of his body lined up with hers sent waves of heat up and down her front.

He slid a hand around the back of her neck and angled her head to the side, pulling her down so that he murmured against her lips, "I was doing such a good job of ignoring temptation, but you, my love—you are just the sweet droplet needed to push me over the edge."

"What—mph."

He kissed her gently, then again, then thrust his tongue deep, mouth devouring hers.

She clutched at his shoulders, reaching, arching closer, hands stroking, trying desperately to get closer.

They lost themselves in long heat-filled moments until

the sound of a loud throat clearing broke them apart and they looked up to see Bryce standing over them, hands on his hips, an incredulous look on his face.

"I go away for two days and the world's gone mad! What the hell is going on around here? That is you, Lumiki, right?"

She groaned and slowly lifted her head from where she'd buried it against Zach's chest the moment she'd realized who was standing over them. "Yes. It's me, Bryce."

"So you and Zach are dating now?"

"Uh—"

"We actually think we're mates," Zach said quietly.

The look on Bryce's face was nothing less than stunned.

Lumiki thought that was an appropriate response, considering it was how she'd felt when she'd come to the same conclusion.

"But that—that's fantastic! Congratulations, you two!" Bryce beamed at them.

"Thanks," they chorused.

He scowled at them. "But let's not get in the habit of making out in my office. Got it?" He glanced around. "And why in the name of all the goddesses is my office full of cat stuff and *cats?*"

ZACH WAS STILL CHUCKLING HOURS LATER WHEN he remembered the look on Bryce's face as he realized his office had been transformed into a cat utopia.

He still wasn't convinced Bryce wouldn't strangle Isana the next time he saw her, especially once he'd heard how Bryce had spent his two days off.

Apparently Isana had delivered a cat to Bryce's house over the weekend.

A cat she'd been attempting to adopt out for the past year.

A cat they'd all heard numerous stories about.

A cat named Shredder.

The Shredder.

The cat who had been rejected by *seventeen* human families because he was misunderstood (according to Isana) or because he was a raging asshole (according to Bryce).

If Zach were taking bets, he'd lay odds on the latter.

Apparently, Isana felt Bryce was the perfect candidate for adopting the psychotic cat.

So then to discover Isana was insisting they also take care of cats at his work was probably enough to send Bryce over the edge.

Zach grinned.

He was definitely going to enjoy watching the fireworks.

Though he'd make sure the kittens and their mama wouldn't suffer any consequences from the fallout since they were so cute.

Especially the little white kitten, who had spent the majority of the day with him in the kitchen.

When she hadn't been perched on his shoulder, nuzzling his ear or chewing his hair, she'd been sitting on his shoes, chewing on his shoelaces or climbing his trousers.

When she hadn't been actively attached to him in some way, she'd been racing up and down the counter where he was working or sleeping in a bowl nearby.

He'd tried keeping her off his workstation, but she just didn't seem to understand the concept of down or stay or no. And she never really stayed in one place for long.

The other kittens came around too, and sometimes she would go off with them, but more often than not, she'd come right back.

She was definitely the cutest of the lot.

And speaking of cute, it had taken him all night, but he'd come up with a plan and it was now time to launch Campaign Adoption.

He'd recruited Luke's assistance and he'd finally arrived with all the necessary materials—tiny chef hats and Polaroid cameras.

Zach had also recruited the entire kitchen staff, including Steve, though he hadn't been thrilled at first.

"Why is there a kitten in my kitchen?" he'd roared, loudly enough that Lumiki had come running.

Zach had just waved her off, not wanting her to catch on too soon to his plans.

Eventually, Zach managed to calm Steve down and with

the promise of new pastry gadgets, had even gotten him to allow the orange, tiger-striped kitten to pose next to one of his pastries that he'd claimed was flawed and couldn't possibly be served to the public.

The calm lasted only until he realized Zach was taking a picture to memorialize the moment forever.

Then Steve freaked out.

"What do you mean you took a picture of it? It's flawed!" he roared. "It needs to be destroyed! Never to be seen or consumed or acknowledged. Erased from existence. Not snapshotted onto a piece of paper to be captured forever, immortalized. What is wrong with you?"

He looked to be about two seconds from transforming into his bear, which would be a true disaster for The Ice Box.

"Okay, Steve. Calm down," Zach said. "It's not flawed. Actually it's quite perfect. I've never seen a more beautiful pastry. If there is a flaw, it's the flaw that makes it perfect."

Steve froze in his frantic pacing to stare at Zach. "How can a flaw make anything perfect?"

"Because perfection is a flaw in itself. How can anything perfect be anything but flawed?"

"That doesn't make any sense."

"Something perfect has tried entirely too hard to achieve perfection. Therefore, it cannot possibly be perfect. It must be flawed. Anything perfect is simply trying too hard. There has to be a flaw somewhere that cannot be seen. It is the flaws that we see that tell us something is truly perfect."

"That is completely—ridiculously—absurdly—outrageously—profoundly—"

"Perfect?"

Steve sighed, scooped up the kitten and handed him to Zach, along with the Polaroid. "Go away now. You're exhausting and I need to get back to work."

Zach grinned. "You got it. Thanks, Steve."

And so it went. Zach and the rest of the kitchen staff continued cooking and capturing the moments with the kittens, until a few hours later, armed with a handful of Polaroids, Zach was finally ready for Operation Adoption.

"WHAT IN THE WORLD IS GOING ON HERE?" KALYN exclaimed, glaring at the earthbound kitten currently sitting happily on Zach's shoulder. "You're fraternizing with the enemy!"

The kitten turned her head and licked the polar's ear.

"Clearly she likes *this* polar bear," Gwyneira said.

The bear chuckled and scratched the white kitten's chin.

"Ugh," Kalyn groaned. "Earthbound cats are so unreliable."

"Oh, don't give up yet. They're just getting started. Besides, as long as this polar's in the kitchen, he's not out there flirting with Lumiki."

Kalyn brightened. "I guess that's true. Huh. Hadn't thought of it like that. Good work then. Keep him distracted in here while the other kittens work on getting Lumiki and Wade together out there. Yes, that will work just fine. I like this plan."

He looked around the room.

"Except we need the other kittens out there then. Hey there! All of you kittens! Time to get out there and start working on the romance between Lumiki and Wade! Remember them? The *other* polar bear and the arctic fox? Get to it then. Mistletoe kisses? Ringing any bells? Come along now!"

"Oh, for heaven's sake." Gwyneira produced a strand of mistletoe and waved it in the air. "Come along, kitties. Time to play." She ran through the kitchen and out the door.

ZACH SELECTED TWO POLAROIDS TO START WITH and grabbed a couple plates intended for table seven.

As he headed for the swinging doors to the dining room, two kittens, followed by a third leapt into his path and barreled out the doors.

He stumbled to a halt, then shook his head as a fourth kitten streaked by.

He tilted his head to glance down at little Snowball, who

was still perched on his left shoulder, calmly giving herself a bath.

She seemed oblivious to the antics of her siblings and instead turned her attentions to the Ice Box logo on his shirt, leaning down to bat at it with her front paws.

She was obsessed with that logo.

He had no idea why.

It was just the words The Ice Box one on top of the other, but there was an arctic fox peeking out from behind the word Box and a polar bear lying across the whole thing and the kitten seemed obsessed with trying to detach one or the other, never mind that neither was going anywhere.

Zach chuckled, shook his head and strode out, careful in his movements not to dislodge the playful kitten who continued to bat and gnaw at the characters on his shirt.

Arriving at table seven, he delivered their meals with a flourish, announcing, "Your meals today were prepared by Chef Brogan and his assistant, a tiny homeless kitten we've named Chef Z. Please let us know if you'd be interested in applying to adopt this adorable black kitten for your very own." He then offered them each a Polaroid of the kitten, who was sporting a tiny chef hat in each picture. In one picture, he was curled up inside a serving bowl fast asleep and in the other, he was batting at a serving spoon Chef Brogan was wielding.

Leaving the diners with grins on their faces, Zach turned and sauntered away, feeling quite smug in his adoption efforts.

Glancing around the room, hoping Lumiki had observed his performance, he came to a screeching halt when he realized that in addition to *not* witnessing his elaborate sales pitch, she was also hanging out at the bar with *Wade.*

Worse, she appeared to be *leaning* toward him.

LUMIKI ALMOST TRIPPED WHEN A KITTEN RAN right in front of her path, followed by three others. "Well, my goodness! Where are you four going in such a hurry?"

She watched, hands on hips, as they made a beeline for Wade, not surprised to see that a certain white kitten was missing. Probably hanging with a cranky bear who claimed he had no use for kittens.

Lumiki chuckled, glanced around and decided things looked calm enough she could probably take a few minutes to cuddle a kitten or two. She headed for the bar where all four kittens were being given plenty of attention by another bear making the same claim.

These bears.

So completely oblivious to their downfalls.

Isana was a pure genius.

Wade looked up and grinned at Lumiki.

"I know what you're thinking," he said, "but you're wrong."

Lumiki grinned and settled her arms on the bar, leaned forward and stroked a hand down the back of one of the tabbies. "Okay, I'll bite. What am I thinking?"

"You're thinking we're going to end up keeping these kittens and their mama too."

"Well. I'm pretty sure it's a done deal where Zach and a certain white fluff ball is concerned."

Wade looked up and let out a bark of laughter.

Lumiki glanced over her shoulder and saw Zach walking across the restaurant with the white fluff ball in question on his shoulder. She giggled and looked back at Wade. "See what I mean?"

"Yeah, I'm sure you're right on that one."

"And honestly, you're looking pretty attached to those two."

Wade looked surprised, then glanced down at the two tabbies currently purring under his hands. They were a mix of gray and brown with adorable marbled markings. "Well, I—uh."

At that moment, one of the kittens jumped up onto Lumiki's shoulder, startling her. "Well, hello there." The kitten nuzzled her cheek, set its paws on her head and then set something there before jumping down.

As Lumiki reached up to touch her head, she realized one of the other kittens had done the same thing to Wade.

"What in the world?" She pulled something off her head. It looked like— "Mistletoe?" Horror widened her eyes. She lifted it to her nose. "Thank god it's fake. Mistletoe is toxic to cats."

Wade let out a snort. "I don't think it's fake."

"What?" Lumiki gasped.

"I mean, it may be fake mistletoe, but I'm pretty certain it's full of very real catnip." He nodded toward the other end of the bar where the black kitten and the other tabby—this one an orange, tiger-striped one—were rolling and drooling over a mess of catnip mistletoe.

As they watched, the two tabbies joined their siblings in the rolling and drooling.

"Oh great!" Kalyn exclaimed. "They're freaking high! Did you have to get the catnip-infused mistletoe?"

"Well, I needed to entice them somehow, didn't I?" Gwyneira glared down at the bar. "And we definitely didn't want to poison the poor things. So maybe I should have gone a little lighter on the catnip. Sorry. At least they're having a good time."

"And why didn't it work?" Kalyn demanded. "Where's the kissing? All I'm seeing is a bunch of drooling!"

"I have no idea. This is *not* the normal reaction to mistletoe, even the catnip-infused kind!"

Zach stormed across the restaurant and arrived at the bar just in time to hear one of the bar patrons exclaim, "Hey, is that mistletoe? What are you doing, dummy? Kiss her already!"

Zach's eyes widened as he realized both Lumiki and Wade were holding mistletoe in their hands.

He let out a roar that cut through the entire restaurant.

Lumiki swung around, hands out. "Now, Zach."

Wade threw up his hands and took s step back from the bar. "Dude. Not doing this again. It's a catnip toy, not real mistletoe."

Lumiki grinned. "I'll use it as real mistletoe with you, Zachariah." She crooked her finger at him. "Just get a little closer."

Zach growled and stepped closer to Lumiki, never taking his eyes off Wade the entire time. He slid his arm around her waist, narrowed his eyes at Wade, just daring him to try and steal his prize, then at the very last moment, dropped his eyes to Lumiki, lifted her and claimed her mouth in a sweeping, breathtaking kiss that went on and on and on until he thought they both might pass out from lack of breath and sheer heat.

He finally set her down on her feet, braced one hand on

the bar behind her and held her upright against him until they were both steady on their feet again.

He raised his eyes to Wade again and glared. "Mine."

Wade grinned and held up his hands in surrender. "No problem. All yours. Happy for you both."

Six

"AND THERE'S YOUR kissing," Gwyneira said.

"*Not* the kissing I was looking for," Kalyn said gloomily.

"I know, but it's not like fate's gonna make things easy for us. I mean, we are interfering with destined mates and all that."

"Oh, please."

Gwyneira snickered.

"Like that bear would have ever figured things out without Bygul's interference. The timing was impeccable."

"I'm sorry. Was that—did you just—I could have sworn you just *complimented* your brother."

"Oh, don't be ridiculous. Bygul may be arrogant and an ass, but there's no denying he's very good at his job. He manipulated the entire situation." Kalyn began stalking back and forth, tail swishing madly. "Somehow he managed to get the restaurant to foster an entire litter of earthbound cats and in the process a bear who had never even noticed his mate to actually recognize her!"

"Yeah, that was pretty amazing."

He stopped pacing and glared at Gwyneira, tail still twitching angrily. "Bygul's only problem was he woke the wrong bear. Or at least not the one he was expecting. Either way, it was a bit of brilliant luck. I have no idea how he does it and it drives me mad. Even when he screws up, everything comes out golden!

"And now here we are, Gwyneira, trying to make the match he *should* have made, between the wrong bear and the wrong fox and nobody's cooperating!"

"Right, well, perhaps all isn't lost. After all, he has no idea that Wade isn't the right bear."

"So, what are you suggesting?"

"That we tell Bygul *Zach* is attempting to steal his cousin's mate."

Kalyn's tail froze mid-swish. "But that would be so very —*wrong*. Really, *really* wrong."

Gwyneira's ears quivered, a sign of pure anticipation.

"I love it!"

THE NEXT COUPLE WEEKS WERE THE MOST amazing—and strangest—of Lumiki's life.

Amazing because she and Zach spent those two weeks getting to know each other, not as lifetime friends or as coworkers, but as mates.

They continued trying to outwit each other by convincing customers to apply to adopt kittens. Each time one of them accepted an application for a kitten—and by the time the holidays came around, they had quite a stack for Isana—they had to pay a forfeit, which ran from a creative date to an incredibly heated kissing session.

Some of those dates were as simple as picnic and long walks in the woods together. Some were more elaborate like revisiting places from their youth, including the Greensboro Diner, where Zach and occasionally Bryce had enjoyed ruining Lumiki and Isana's dating lives.

As the holidays approached, they did began to do more traditional things together like Christmas shopping for friends and family, which was quite an experience because neither of them enjoyed shopping so their excursion ended up more like a mission to get in and out as quickly as possible.

As they moved down their list, each name turned into a contest between them to see who would be the quickest at finding that person the perfect gift.

Of course, their definitions of perfect were rarely in alignment.

Zach would shake his head at Lumiki's gift, then say,

"You're right. It's perfect. They'll love it, I'm sure." Then he would bring out his gift, which would either make Lumiki blush or close her eyes in horror or possibly shake her head in confusion.

Invariably, his explanation would leave her in stitches and in the end, more often than not, they would end up buying both gifts because somehow together, the two gifts became absolutely perfect.

It was during this shopping expedition that Lumiki realized she didn't know Zach at all.

After all, hadn't she just been saying to Isana that Zach was too serious for her?

She wanted to conclude he had all these hidden depths to him, but these gifts were ones he was giving to family and friends, and she'd been participating in family events for years, so how had she missed this part of his personality?

Had she just been that oblivious, that completely unaware?

She texted Isana that very question and got a bunch of laughing emojis back followed by "Zach *is* a stick-in-the-mud or have you forgotten all the dates he ruined when we were in high school and college?"

Lumiki rolled her eyes.

Valid point, but still.

It hit her kind of hard, realizing she'd apparently judged Zach fairly harshly, tarnishing him with that one brush, all of it based on that one experience—okay, one experience over *tons* of dates—and had never allowed that judgment to change until now.

When she tried to apologize to Zach, though, he just laughed and kissed her breathless and reminded her that he'd been oblivious too. "Bears. I don't even have an excuse. You weren't a jerk, keeping me from dating other girls. You were always there, sweet as can be. I just never saw you for my mate because I'm an idiot. And a bear." Then he kissed her again, sending heat rushing through her once more.

And so, the beautiful days marched on, leading them closer to Christmas and the new year.

As they got closer, of course, things got busier and crazier at the restaurant with holiday parties and last-minute bookings and late nights and early mornings and of course, their continued half-hearted attempts to find homes for the kittens.

Half-hearted because Lumiki really wanted them to be their restaurant kitties and Zach had clearly fallen in love with the little kitten he called Snowball and had begun to mellow toward the other kittens as well.

Zach had ramped up his Polaroid sales pitches, which were becoming increasingly ridiculous, forcing Lumiki to follow behind him with disclaimers.

"So, Mrs. Robinson," Zach said, "how would you like an adorable black kitten with your dessert today? No? Then, how about this sweet little tiger-striped beauty?"

"I'm sorry, Mrs. Robinson," Lumiki explained, glaring at Zach's back as he moved on to the next table, "but we're not really offering kittens with desserts. I'm afraid you must apply if you'd like to adopt any kittens. Applications are at the hostess stand."

She arrived at the next table just in time to hear Zach say, "Kitten with your glass of Chardonnay this evening?" He was driving her crazy. "No? Are you sure?"

"No kittens come with the wine, I apologize. Applications are at the hostess stand." Lumiki smiled at the diners, then hurried to catch up with Zach. "Would you stop it already?"

"What? I'm just trying to win our wager."

"Oh, give me a break. I notice you haven't offered any Polaroids of a certain white kitten yet."

"I don't know what you're talking about."

"Snowball?"

Zach scowled at her. "Who—" he broke off when a tiny white head peeked out of Zach's apron pocket.

Lumiki giggled. "Hello, darling. Are you keeping Zach company? I'm surprised she still fits in there."

Zach sighed. "She won't for much longer."

"You might as well give it up. You know she's yours."

"If I apply to adopt her, Isana wins. She'll know that I'm a sucker and then she can get me to take in animals whenever she wants."

"She forced Bryce to take in Shredder. Maybe we can get her to force you to adopt Snowball. You can act all reluctant and be the martyr and she'll never know you actually want Snowball for your own."

Zach eyed Lumiki. "You're as devious as she is."

"Why do you think we're best friends?" Lumiki grinned as she hurried toward the hostess stand. She had so much to do and nowhere near enough time for everything.

There had been parties every night this week plus—

Not again.

Catnip mistletoe freaking everywhere.

She had no idea where the stuff was coming from.

It just kept appearing.

It now covered her hostess stand and it was driving her crazy.

As she went to pull it off the stand, a wolf shifter approached, a wide grin on his face. "Mistletoe kisses."

She held up a hand. "No."

"Ah, come on, 'tis the season."

"No. My mate will not approve."

"But you're not claimed."

"Still have a mate."

"Just a small one?"

"No."

"No tongue."

"No."

"Come on. It's mistletoe!"

She sighed. "What do you not understand about the word no?"

He groaned. "Fine. Whatever." He turned and slouched back toward his party of four. The others he was with just laughed and slapped him on the back.

Lumiki rolled her eyes and continued disassembling the catnip mistletoe.

It had become the bane of her existence.

Four more customers approached before she got it all taken down.

Unfortunately, Zach, who had retreated to the kitchen, was back in the dining room when the fourth customer approached.

"You need to go away now," Lumiki warned the lion shifter. "My mate has spotted you and he isn't happy."

The lion shifter just shrugged. "I'm not worried."

"You should be."

"Look. If you didn't want to be offered kisses, you shouldn't decorate the hostess stand in mistletoe, that's all I'm saying. You gotta see my point here, right? I mean, come on. You literally covered your work space in a giant invitation that says 'KISS ME' and now you're upset that people are asking for a kiss? It doesn't make sense, love."

He kind of had a point.

So now Lumiki was feeling kind of bad.

"Look, the thing is, I didn't decorate the hostess stand. I'm not sure how the mistletoe keeps appearing and it feels like a very nasty practical joke. Either that or god magic and either way, I'm not very happy about it. So, I'm sorry, I really am, but I didn't extend the invitation. Someone else did, without my permission and it's got me rather upset, you see? And worse, it has my polar bear mate upset and he's heading this way."

The lion's eyes got big. "I see." He took a big step back. "I apologize. I didn't realize exactly what was going on. Perhaps, if I might make a suggestion, a sign would be a good idea, explaining the situation. That might help."

That was actually a really good idea. "Thank you. That's an excellent idea." Lumiki hurried around the stand and got between the lion and an approaching Zach. "I'll distract him, then you can head back to your table."

He nodded. "Good luck."

Lumiki waited until Zach was a couple paces away, then flung herself at him.

He caught her in his arms and she wrapped herself around him, arms and legs clenching tight so that she clung to him like a burr. "Hi, Zach. Wanna kiss me under the mistletoe?" She showed him the strand she was holding in her hand, then held it over their heads, and planted her mouth on his.

He took over the kiss immediately, driving his tongue deep, one hand on her ass, kneading gently, the other hand holding her head steady, sifting through the hair at the back of her head, heat barreling through her, making everything in her tighten in breathless anticipation.

ZACH FOUND THE FOLLOWING TWO WEEKS TO BE absolutely wonderful and strange all at the same time.

Wonderful because he was with his mate and she was the best thing that had ever happened to him.

No matter what they were doing or where they were, he felt incredibly blessed to be with her. He enjoyed Christmas shopping with her and exploring their town with her, but he especially enjoyed reenacting all those dates he had ruined for her so many years before.

A highlight for him was kissing her in all those places so many idiots he'd hated back in the day had wanted to kiss her, but had been too chicken to do so under his angry stare.

Every single time, she would giggle and kiss him back, and he would know in that moment, *this* was what he'd wanted back then, all those years before.

He hadn't understood.

Not then.

His bear hadn't understood.

But he'd been standing guard.

While she'd been dating idiots, he'd been standing guard over his mate, waiting for her to see him, waiting for his bear to see her, waiting for this moment right here.

Waiting for her.

Such wonderful moments.

They were also strange times because of what was happening at the restaurant.

Busy and crazy because of the holidays.

But strange because of the cats.

Mistletoe catnip kept showing up everywhere. Mostly in the bar, but pretty much everywhere.

And no one would admit they were buying it and bringing it into the restaurant.

Zach and Lumiki kept throwing it away and it kept showing up again.

Nothing they did got rid of it.

It seemed to follow Lumiki around.

Every time she turned around, it was there, and the customers were taking advantage.

It was driving Zach stark, raving mad.

Every time he turned around, some bastard shifter was trying to kiss his mate!

He was constantly threatening to tear shifters limb from limb, fat lot of good that did.

They always claimed innocence in the form of mistletoe. As if that gave them the right to touch a mated shifter.

"Unclaimed," they said.

Whatever.

Not okay!

As if that wasn't bad enough, his own cousins and brother were getting involved as well.

It was enough to make a shifter go bonkers!

Even Wade had started kissing Lumiki on the cheek anytime he spotted mistletoe near her. You'd think he'd learned his lesson after Zach tossed him across the lobby, but no. Wade seemed to think it was funny to torture Zach.

Then, Bryce and Steve got involved.

As if that wasn't bad enough, Luke was on the schedule to fill in this week, so now he was part of the torture as well.

Where was the loyalty?

Apparently it didn't exist anymore!

So wrong!

He couldn't kill family, unfortunately, but there was nothing protecting customers from his wrath. This was the only thing keeping Zach's sanity intact and he was simply waiting for the moment when he was able to catch a customer in the act.

So far, everyone had conspired against him.

Family and employees working together to protect the customers, but they couldn't possibly keep that up for long. Eventually, he would catch one of them in the act and they would pay the price.

He had a good feeling about today.

A very good feeling.

Then it happened.

A lion shifter was all up in his Lumiki's space, clearly attempting to coerce some of Zach's mistletoe kisses from his mate.

Zach was full of so much anticipation and glee as he stormed across the restaurant.

He had every intention of beating that lion shifter to death, but then Lumiki distracted him with her foxy ways and sexy scent and mistletoe kisses and the damn lion got away.

Zach wanted to be furious, but all his anger drained

south along with all the blood in his body. Every beat of his heart, every breath in his lungs, every rush of blood in his veins had one simple purpose: *Lumiki.*

"YOU KNOW THOSE KITTENS MAY NEVER BE USEFUL members of society after this," Kalyn observed.

Four of the five earthbound kittens were currently sprawled on the bar in The Ice Box in a tangle of limbs.

The brown, marbled tabbies were curled around each other, clutching sprigs of mistletoe between them.

The black kitten was sprawled on its back, on top of a bed of mistletoe, all four limbs spread wide.

The orange, tiger-striped tabby was between the marbled tabbies and the black kitten, curled in a ball with a sprig of mistletoe clutched between its paws under its chin.

"Eh, they'll still be cute," Gwyneira said.

"Cute little addicts, you mean."

"Oh, I wouldn't worry about that. Mama cat's gonna cut them off, any minute now."

"Really?"

Gwyneira just nodded toward the kittens.

A moment later, the mama cat jumped onto the bar, walked over to the kittens and calmly smacked each one awake, nudged them off the catnip, swept all the mistletoe into a pile, then stretched out on top of it and glared at the kittens as if daring them to try and take the mistletoe away from her.

Kalyn snorted. "Well, that's an interesting development."

"Hey. Mama needs some stress relief too, probably way more than the little ones."

Lumiki was so ready for this day to be finished, but there was a party tonight and then—

"Hey, Lumiki! Mistletoe!"

"Oh, hey, Luke. So you're on again tonight, huh?"

"Yep. Every night this week for the parties. Thank goodness tomorrow's Christmas Eve and this crazy madness will begin to wind down. What's up with all the mistletoe?"

"I have no idea. It's driving me crazy."

He grinned at her. "Well, you know who else it's driving crazy?"

She sighed. "Zach?"

"Exactly. And I promised Wade I'd do my best to mess with him."

"What? Why?"

"Eh, something about tossing him across the room and mates and I don't even know what."

"Oh, for heaven's sake."

"So, come on, lay it on me."

"What?"

"Give me your best cousinly kiss, right here." He tapped his cheek. "Or here." He tapped his lips. "Or here." He tapped his forehead. "Wherever you prefer, princess."

She rolled her eyes. "Why?"

"Because we're messing with Zach. And—" he pointed up. "Mistletoe."

She glanced up and saw there was mistletoe hanging from every single light fixture in the dining room. "Oh my goddess. How in the hell? Someone is going to pay."

"Come on, Lumiki. Or would you prefer me to kiss you? I can totally make it a good one."

"Luke, if Zach throws you across the room the way he did Wade, it's your own fault and I will not offer you one iota of sympathy."

"Understood. Hold up. We've got to get this lined up perfectly." He set his hands on her shoulders and maneuvered her so that she was directly under the light fixture. "Perfect."

"Why the hell are we doing this again?"

"Because we're family and family messes with family. It's tradition. Ready, Wade?" He raised his voice on the last two words.

"Ready!" Wade called from across the room.

"Wait. What? What's going on?" Lumiki started to turn

around, but Luke caught her by the shoulders and stilled her movement.

"Ah-ah-ah. Stay right where you are. Okay. You know what? Forgive me, darling, but I think we should just go for it." He let go of her shoulders, stepped back, cleared his throat, stepped forward and in one sweeping move, grabbed her around the waist, bent her back over his arm, planted a swift kiss on her mouth, then swept her upright again.

It all happened so fast, she was left speechless at the end of it, and the only way she actually knew it had happened was because the entire restaurant broke out into applause when it was over.

She swayed in place when Luke let her go.

"Whoa, you okay?"

"Um, yeah. What the hell was that, Luke?"

He laughed. "Just a little fun to torture Zach with."

"Got it all recorded right here." Wade waved his phone as he walked up to join them.

Lumiki groaned. "Are you freaking insane? You are, aren't you? Oh my goddess, Zach is going to kill us all."

"What the hell's going on out here?"

Wonderful. Because all it needed was her insanely jealous mate to join the party.

Wade grinned gleefully and pointed up. "Lumiki and Luke ended up under the mistletoe at the same time."

Zach scowled, reached out and yanked Lumiki into his arms. "She's mine." He glared at Luke.

Lumiki grabbed his hand and pulled him toward the

kitchen. "Of course I'm yours, Zach. Everyone knows that. They're just trying to rile you up. Come on." She pointed at them behind his back and made a stabbing motion at her throat, threatening to decapitate them if Zach ever saw that video.

They just grinned back at her.

Bastards!

Seven

"YOU KNOW, THIS has become quite the interesting match," Gwyneira said.

"It really has," Kalyn said. "I did not expect things to go this way at all, especially not with the cats."

"I know. I'm especially surprised at the tiger-striped one."

"And the mama."

"SO THE THING ABOUT THE *MILLE-FEUILLE* IS IT IS made with pastry cream, not almond cream like the Napoleon. It's an important distinction, you see, my little

Cream Puff, because it will not taste quite right if you use the wrong ingredient."

Zach paused outside the pastry kitchen and listened as his cousin Steve described the dessert he was currently working on to no one as far as he could tell.

Steve enjoyed working alone and for as long as Zach could remember, never spoke to anyone while working unless it was to bark at one of the workers to carry one of Steve's creations to the pass, where it would eventually be carried onto the floor for consumption.

There were other workers in the pastry kitchen, but Steve never acknowledged them and they never interrupted his work, so this was highly unusual.

The other workers in the pastry kitchen kept throwing glances Steve's way, but none of them responded to his comments, thus Zach was pretty sure Steve was not addressing any of them.

Perhaps he was speaking to someone via Bluetooth. The problem was Zach couldn't imagine anyone in Steve's life that he would address as my little cream puff.

Unless he'd met his mate.

Or he'd finally lost his mind.

Zach grimaced.

He hated to think, but it was probably the latter. It seemed almost inevitable.

Feeling an almost overwhelming sense of dread, he stepped into the pastry kitchen, dragged in a deep breath and walked around the center island, toward the back wall where Steve was working on his precious *mille-feuille* desserts.

He was about halfway there when he realized the orange tabby was stretched out on Steve's work station and that Steve was having a full-fledged conversation with that kitten.

"So, you see, sweet Ambrosia, there are supposed to be one thousand leaves on this particular dessert. Interpreting that as a thousand pastry sheets, that would be six folds of three puff pastry layers, with of course, two layers of pastry cream between. It's an awful lot of work, but still doable. What do you think, my dear?" He paused as if waiting for her to answer, then nodded as if she had in fact answered. "I agree. It is a lot of work, but trust me, the end result is well worth it."

Zach was simply frozen in place, unable to believe what he was seeing.

The kitten, Creme Puff or Ambrosia or whatever, seemed mesmerized, listening to Steve share all his wisdom about pastries and Steve was actually communicating and working and seemed quite calm and content.

For a split second, Zach was certain he'd entered an alternate dimension, then for another second, he was certain Steve was just messing with him in the same way that Wade and Luke had been messing with him just moments before, but then Lumiki was suddenly at his side, grabbing his hand and ushering him back out the way they'd come.

They left the pastry kitchen behind, then walked through the regular kitchen as well.

This time, Zach took note of the looks on everyone's faces.

He hadn't noticed when walking through before, but now he did. Everyone looked like they were waiting for the other shoe to drop, like they expected at any moment for someone to go psycho on them.

He now knew they were waiting on Steve because what they had just seen was *not* normal.

They left the kitchens behind and headed for the office.

Lumiki dragged him into the office and Zach slammed the office door behind them, then collapsed against it.

Bryce was standing at his desk, looking through receipts and jerked his head up when Zach slammed the door. "What's the matter?"

"Something's wrong with Steve," Zach said. "He's acting psycho."

Lumiki pulled away and smacked Zach on the arm. "He is not. That was so sweet. What is wrong with you?"

"Sweet! Are you kidding me right now? Any minute, we could be smelling kitty-cat pie."

Lumiki gasped. "You're horrible! Steve would *never*!"

"All right. What's going on?" Bryce demanded.

"Steve was talking to one of the kittens," Zach said. "He was having an entire conversation with her, about pastries and ingredients and—and—I don't know—stuff."

"It was sweet," Lumiki insisted. "I think we should let him adopt the kitten, but have the kitten stay here as a restaurant kitty, that way we know the kitten is being taken care of and Steve can have a companion. It will help him develop empathy and compassion, not to mention communication skills."

"Communication skills?" Zach scoffed. "The kitten won't communicate back. It'll all be one-sided."

"So? Right now Steve doesn't communicate with anybody. One-sided is better than zero-sided."

Bryce sighed. "Fine. I'll talk with Isana. If she agrees, the kitten can stay."

"Yay!" Lumiki clapped and jumped up and down.

Zach scowled. "For the record, I think this is a terrible idea."

Lumiki rolled her eyes. "Of course, you do. I'm not sure Steve will actually agree to adopt the kitten. Isana might just have to give the kitten to him, or to the restaurant I should say, since he wasn't exactly open to the idea when I approached him about it a couple weeks ago."

Bryce sighed. "I'll see what she says. You know she's completely opposed to giving pets as gifts."

Lumiki frowned at him. "Didn't she just give *you* a cat?"

"Yeah, well. Apparently those rules don't apply to *her*."

ZACH SCOWLED AT LUMIKI AS THEY WALKED DOWN the hall toward the kitchens. "Traitor."

"Hey. What'd I do?"

"You're supposed to be setting things up so that Isana gifts me Snowball and instead you're setting things up so that Psycho Steve gets his precious Cream Puff. How is that helping out your mate?"

"I'm just setting the stage. Don't worry. I've got you covered."

"You'd better." He hooked an arm around her neck, pulled her into a shadowy corner of the hallway and kissed her breathless.

Long moments later, he set her loose and sauntered off into the kitchen.

It took her a few moments to recover her breath before she headed back into the dining room.

Dear goddess, he was potent.

She was so ready for him to claim her and to be mated for real.

At this point, she had no idea why they were waiting.

Tomorrow was Christmas Eve.

Soon enough, they'd be starting a new year.

She was determined to enter it a mated woman.

Better yet, she'd like to wake up that way on Christmas morning.

Tonight they had yet another party, so it would be a very long night.

Then tomorrow was the restaurant's annual Christmas Eve party. It would be utter madness, an all hands on deck type of event that would mean an even longer night.

Then finally Christmas Day.

Which in the restaurant world finally meant a day off.

Of course, it was also the Meiers' annual Christmas Day bash, which was at Bryce's house this year, which, now that Lumiki thought about it, meant that Bryce would have tomorrow off.

She groaned.

Zach was great at his job, he just wasn't Bryce, which meant things were sure to go sideways a little faster than usual without their fearless leader to keep things running smoothly.

Just thinking of all the things Lumiki needed to accomplish in the next couple days had tiny tendrils of panic beginning to swirl deep inside.

And her parents!

At some point, Christmas morning, she would have to find time to swing by her parents' house to mention to them that Zach Meier was her mate.

She had to do that *before* they all showed up at Bryce's house and they discovered it while surrounded by the entire Meier clan.

She could hear her parents now, berating her because they were the last ones to know.

She'd been expecting them to call and ask her about Zach for the last couple weeks since they'd been seen together all over the place, but they hadn't, so she was going to have to bring it up herself.

Joy.

Yet another thing on her plate to look forward to.

Shaking off her thoughts that were accomplishing nothing but to send her deeper into panic, Lumiki headed into the dining room and forward into her day of madness.

The rest of the afternoon and evening passed in a flurry of activity.

Demanding customers.

Mistletoe kisses.

Rampaging bear roars.

Airborne diners.

Collapsed tables.

Kittens high on catnip.

Exhausted employees.

And entirely too many inebriated customers stuck in their animal forms, having had one too many shots of The Beast Within.

"I knew we shouldn't have stocked that damn drink," Bryce muttered.

"Hey, it's a high price item," Wade said. "We make great profit on it and it literally flies off the shelf."

"Sure, but it results in endless aggravations at the end of the night," Zach said.

"Yeah, and they're mostly wolves," Bryce said, glaring at the howling idiots at table five.

"Eh, wolves are idiots, no matter what they drink, and if it's a full moon, forget it," Wade said.

"Cars are lining up," Lumiki announced from her spot

by the window where she'd been monitoring the car service stand outside.

"Excellent," Bryce said. "Let's get 'em out of here."

An hour later, the last of the party-goers were finally gone and they were all collapsed in the main dining room, feeling like they'd been run over by a semi.

"Why do we do this to ourselves?" Zach asked. "Why do we do parties? We could just not do them. We make enough money to just run the restaurant. It's not like we have to do the parties."

Bryce shrugged. "Because we make a lot of bank."

"A *lot* of bank," Wade said. "And it means excellent Christmas bonuses for *everyone.*"

"Oh. Right. That's why."

They all fell silent.

Lumiki knew this truly was the reason. Because none of the owners, even those who only owned about ten percent needed the extra money from the parties. Instead, the profit from the parties went entirely to their hourly employees, so those like Lumiki could enjoy some of the blessings of working for a successful restaurant at least once a year.

And that was why Lumiki continued working for The Ice Box year after year.

Because at the end of the day, The Ice Box, truly was a family-run business.

Christmas Eve dawned bright and cold.

Lumiki woke with a groan.

Her entire body hurt.

She hobbled to the bathroom, feeling like a little old lady.

She stood under the shower, waiting for it to wake her up, glaring down at her feet. "You're supposed to get me from point A to B, not punish me for it. Why do you whine so much? It's not right, I tell you."

She was standing in her kitchen, contemplating breakfast, not loving her choices, when there came a knock at the door.

"Zach!"

"Merry Christmas Eve." He slipped a hand behind her neck, pulled her forward and kissed her.

She clutched his shoulders, leaned in and kissed him back.

He slid an arm around her waist, lifted her and stepped forward, closing the door behind them, never breaking contact with her. He leaned back against the door and continued kissing her.

Long, breathless moments later, he slid his lips from hers to trail kisses down her neck to bury his face in her shoulder, where he inhaled deeply and murmured, "My Lumiki. You make me so happy, my love."

She ran her fingers through his white hair, scraping her nails along his scalp and reveled in the way he tensed, then surged against her, groaning her name again. "Zach."

"I came to take you to breakfast," he groaned.

She leaned back. "Let's have breakfast in bed."

His eyes darkened, full of heat. "We only have two hours. That'll never be enough time."

"No, but it'll take the edge off."

"Bryce will kill me."

"Why?"

"Because there's no way after having you that I'll resist dragging you off to his office at some point during the day."

Lumiki giggled. "I'll look forward to it." She sobered and staring into his eyes, whispered, "Please, Zach, make me yours."

"WELL, THIS IS A TOTAL NIGHTMARE!" BYGUL exclaimed. "How could you let this happen?"

"You mean Zach and Lumiki?" Kalyn asked innocently, practically dancing with glee inside.

"Of course, I mean Zach and Lumiki," Bygul exclaimed. "She's supposed to be with Wade. I know I told you Wade!"

"Yes, and we tried to make that happen. The problem is you were wrong, Bygul." Oh, how he loved saying those words.

"Wrong? I'm never wrong!"

"Then why didn't Wade get jealous when his brother Luke kissed her?" Kalyn asked. "Why would he take a video of it to torture his cousin Zach with instead?" He'd thought that was purely genius.

"And why did *Zach* throw *Wade* across the room when Wade touched her, quite innocently I might add?" Gwyneira asked.

Bygul just stared at them. "But Lumiki said *Wade* was her mate. She didn't mention Zach at all."

"And yet, she just invited *Zach* to mate with her," Kalyn said. "Admit it, Bygul, you were wrong."

THERE WAS NO WAY ZACH COULD EVER RESIST such a heartfelt plea from his mate. "Very well. Lead me to your den, sweet fox of mine."

Lumiki clasped his hand in hers and led him through the tiny living quarters into her bedroom.

Zach grinned. It truly was a den.

Dark and cozy

The bed took up most of the room with pillows piled

high and blankets everywhere. He could totally picture his fox in the middle of that bed, cozy and warm.

He spun her toward him, lifted her in his arms and kissed her.

The taste and scent of his mate barreled through him, a thousand times more potent, here in her den, surrounded by her things, her scent permeating everything around them.

It was heady, intoxicating, overwhelming.

"Lumiki."

"Zach," she whispered back, clutching him closer, kissing him back just as fiercely as he was kissing her.

She pulled back and began pulling at his shirt.

At first he didn't understand, he just moved with her to make sure they never lost contact, but then her hand was on his chest and he realized she'd been unbuttoning his shirt.

Oh.

He quickly peeled it away and watched eagerly as she peeled off her own shirt and bra.

Exquisite.

They came back together, both of them groaning at the sensation of skin-on-skin.

They clutched at each other, kissing, stroking, mad with the desire to get closer, closer, before pulling apart to drag their jeans down and kick off their shoes.

They stumbled back and fell onto the bed, rolling across it, gasping in wonder as they discovered each other in new ways.

Zach rolled her beneath him, linked their hands together and staring into her eyes, sank deep.

She arched her back and whispered his name, "Zach."

"Hold on, Lumiki, my love." He slowly pulled back, causing her to whimper at his loss, then surged forward again.

Lumiki let out a cry of pure ecstasy and Zach grinned.

Perfect.

Watching Lumiki's face the entire time, Zach set a hard and fast pace, plunging deep at the exact same angle, ensuring that he rubbed that exact same spot each time, before pulling out then plunging forward again.

The room echoed with her gasps and cries of ecstasy.

She began to climax somewhere around the third time he plunged deep and that orgasm seemed to last forever and then just as it was dying off, another began.

She was strangling his dick with all those lovely contractions.

Goddess.

He closed his eyes, dug deep for control and managed to wring one final orgasm from her before letting go himself.

Lumiki was on fire.

Her entire body was lit from the inside out.

She couldn't think, she couldn't do anything but feel the extreme heat of Zach's cock that burned her from the inside out.

It had a life of its own, moving inside her, rubbing against places she'd never known existed, triggering things inside her that set off explosions that set off other explosions that made it impossible to breathe, impossible to think, impossible to do anything but feel.

She was burning.

Oh, goddess, he was killing her.

Right there.

Rubbing her right there.

She writhed and clutched at the sheets, trying to escape or maybe to get closer or feel it more, oh, goddess, she had no idea.

She wailed because she could do nothing else.

She sobbed and pleaded with him to do something, something, anything.

Oh, goddess, yes.

The ecstasy just went on and on and on.

She was reeling when it was finally over.

Gasping for breath and completely stunned.

Dear goddess.

There were literally no words for what had just happened.

She was blind.

No. Her eyes were just shut.

Were they shut?

They were shut.

She opened her eyes.

The room came back into focus.

Her ceiling.

Zach's gorgeous brown eyes.

Zach.

"Hi." Was that her voice? So hoarse and scratchy.

"Welcome back."

"I think you killed me."

He smiled. "Just a minor death."

She lifted a hand to his cheek. "My Zachariah."

He turned his head and kissed the palm of her hand. "Yours." He then settled down beside her and pulled her into his arms and kissed her thoroughly.

An hour later, they pulled into the parking lot at The Ice Box.

Zach had driven. It was going to be a long day and he had insisted they might as well go in together.

Of course, he was right. From the minute they entered The Ice Box, there wasn't any down time at all, certainly no opportunities for sexy times in the office, which was a definite disappointment.

The afternoon flew by and soon enough, the restaurant was closed and they were racing around, getting ready for the annual Christmas Eve party.

They had about an hour between the closing of the restaurant and the ramping up of preparations for the party and usually during that time, Lumiki would stuff her face with food and rest her feet, but this time, Zach caught her hand, dragged her into Bryce's office, shoved her up against the wall and rocked her world.

He then did it again on the couch and again on Bryce's desk.

Bryce would *not* be happy upon his return.

Though she tried, Lumiki was certain nothing she did was going to completely get rid of the bear/fox sex scent now permeating the office.

Of course, by the time Zach let her go, they were fifteen minutes late for the preparations and of course, the rest of the night, they had to endure endless teasing from Zach's extended family of endless cousins.

The party lasted hours and it wasn't until the wee hours of the morning that Lumiki and Zach stumbled into his house and fell into his bed together.

They were so exhausted, they tumbled right into sleep with barely a kiss goodnight beforehand.

Eight

"WELL, I GUESS all isn't lost," Bygul said. "At least Lumiki has discovered her happily ever after, even if it is with the wrong mate or at least a different one than she expected. However, this is a disaster for poor Wade."

Now that was pure exaggeration. As far as Kalyn could tell, "poor Wade" wasn't hurting for companionship. He didn't seem too worried about his lack of a mate and seemed to be enjoying torturing his cousin with his newfound mated status.

"I'm just going to have to make things up to Wade somehow. We've already managed to set him up with some cat companions—good job there, Kalyn."

Like he'd been trying to do that. Whatever. His goal there had simply been to cause some chaos and he was pretty certain some of those seeds he'd planted would bear fruit at the Christmas party.

Wade was such an easy target.

Just like Kalyn, he enjoyed torturing his family, though Wade was a bit—okay, a lot—less cruel than Kalyn.

Still, Kalyn liked Wade because he had a great sense of humor and lots of fun ideas for how to mess with his cousin Zach.

Christmas morning dawned bright and snow covered.

This was the perfect Christmas surprise for both Lumiki and Zach.

They raced out into the snow, lunged into their animal forms and played for a couple hours, racing back and forth, as polar bear and arctic fox, snow bursting up from their paws, chasing each other and playing games all around his property until they finally collapsed together in a heap to enjoy the feel of the cold snow against their fur.

Pure joy.

Lumiki rolled around in the snow, making snow foxes, swishing her tail and thinking about how much she'd enjoyed the other night and wondering if the heat they'd generated might have melted all this snow.

She peeked over at her polar bear, who was stretched out in the snow on his belly, eyes on her. She stretched languidly and slowly shifted back into her human form.

"Brrr. Are you going to come over here and warm me up, Zachariah?" She trailed a finger down between her breasts. "I was thinking about the other night, thinking this snow might have cooled us down." She traced the same path down between her breasts, but this time leaving a trail of melting snow in her wake.

Zach let out a low growl, then lunged.

He transformed mid-lunge, pressing her deep into the snow, settling on top of her in human form, and captured her mouth in his.

She kissed him back, then lunged upward, wrapping her arms and legs around him and rolling them so that she landed on top. She lifted up, then sank downward, taking him in.

She fell forward and kissed him. Her hair fell in a curtain around them, shielding them from the outer world, creating a small cavern within which only the two of them existed.

She rose and fell slowly, eyes caught in his, lips pressed together, then apart, then together again, a soft and gentle mating, tender and true.

She whispered his name.

He murmured hers back.

A prayer.

A promise.

An unbreakable bond.

THEY DROVE TO HER PARENTS' HOUSE TOGETHER.

Hand-in-hand, they entered her childhood home and broke the news to her parents, who expressed no surprise whatsoever.

"What do you mean it's about time?" Lumiki demanded.

"For heaven's sake, Zach went on a rampage every single time you went on a date from the time you were thirteen years old, Lumiki," her father said. "Anyone with a brain could figure that one out."

Dead silence.

"He did the same with Isana."

"Did he show up at any of Isana's other friends' dates?" her mother asked.

"Well, no, but I'm her *best* friend."

"Did he show up at any of his female cousins' dates?" her father asked.

"Well, no, but they don't live that close."

"They live in Greensboro, Lumiki," her father said. "It's one town over."

Lumiki turned and stared at Zach, whose cheeks were now red as fire.

"I guess I was a little obvious, huh?"

"If you were so obvious, how come *you* didn't know it?"

"I'm a *bear*. We specialize in being oblivious, even when we're being obvious."

Lumiki rolled her eyes. "That makes zero sense."

Lumiki's mother chuckled. "Just accept it, darling. Otherwise, you'll drive yourself crazy trying to find the logic in the utterly illogical."

"Fine. I'm going to blame Wade though."

"Wade?" Zach demanded. "What's he got to do with it?"

"If he hadn't saved me from those bullies, I probably would have realized you were my mate a lot sooner."

"What are you talking about? What bullies?" Zach's voice dropped to a level that didn't bode well for the bullies.

"Never mind. We should get going."

An hour later, Zach was still nagging Lumiki for information about the bullies and what Wade had to do with her not realizing Zach was her mate.

Lumiki had long since realized she should never have mentioned this line of thought because it would not be good if Zach ever found out that she'd once upon a time believed that Wade was her mate.

This was a secret she needed to take to her grave.

Which meant she had to find Isana, the only other person who knew her secret, and ensure her silence.

Like every other Meier family get-together, this one was a little crazy.

It was even crazier because Bryce had also met his mate, a wolf named Jennifer, who lived next door to Bryce and who apparently specialized in driving him crazy. He accused her of trying to assassinate him no less than three times in the first hour of their arrival.

Jennifer just laughed at him and offered him a bear claw, which he took great offense to.

Lumiki had no idea what his problem was.

The bear claws were *delicious*.

Around hour three, Wade decided it would be a great idea to show a video on the screen his brothers set up in Jennifer's front yard.

Lumiki wasn't paying attention. If she had been, she'd probably have assumed it was a holiday video or something.

The first time she had any inkling something was wrong was when Zach let out the most horrendous roar and an entire table of pastries went flying.

Suddenly, everyone was running for cover as two polar bears transformed in the middle of the party.

They stood on their hind legs and roared at each other.

"Oh, great," Isana said. "It's going to be another bear brawl."

Zach, the larger of the two bears, lunged for Luke, but at the last minute, Luke spun, darted into the street and took off running.

Zach let out a bellow of disbelief, then charged after him.

"I can't believe he ran away!" Isana exclaimed.

"I can," Lumiki said. "I'm pretty sure that was the plan all along." She stamped toward Wade who was rolling around on the snow laughing. "I can't believe you two.

What is wrong with you?" She glared down at him, hands on her hips.

Wade chuckled. "Ah, come on, Lumiki. Zach will never catch Luke, you know that."

"That's not that point!"

Even though it was true. Luke was the fastest runner in high school. He won the Shifter State Championships three years in a row and even went to college on a track scholarship so there was no way Zach would ever catch him, which was probably why he was the one elected to kiss Lumiki in the first place, now that she thought about it.

This was clearly a well-thought-out plan.

"You guys suck."

She whirled on Isana. "And you." She grabbed Isana's arm and pulled her away from Wade.

"Hey, what'd I do?"

"I expect you to take my secret to the grave."

"What secret?"

"About Wade."

"Oh, that. Okay. Except, well, it's kind of too late."

"What?"

"I was so excited when you told me about and Zach, I kind of told everyone."

"Everyone who?"

"The cousins."

"What cousins?"

"All of them."

"Oh my god."

"Oh, don't worry about it. It'll be fine."

"Hey, Lumiki. I can't believe you thought Wade was your mate all this time," Ariana, one of Isana fox cousins walked up to say. "I mean, we always thought it was Zach. Why would you think it was Wade?"

"Argh."

"Wait. What?" Wade, who had been walking by right at that moment, froze mid-step and turned to stare at them. Then, obviously having second thoughts, said, "You know what, never mind, forget I was here," and quickly walked away.

Lumiki groaned. "Shoot me now."

An hour later, Lumiki was sitting by the fire surrounded by Meiers, but not her mate, having endured the longest torture round of quizzing known to man.

She'd told the story over and over again about how Wade had rescued her from bullies and her fox had become convinced he was her mate and blah-blah-blah.

She wasn't even sure if it was her fox or if it was her, but she wasn't admitting that. As far as these people were concerned, it was her fox and that was that.

Isana hadn't left her side once, probably because she felt horribly guilty, and she should! She totally should!

Lumiki was dreading when Zach got back.

No matter how bad it was now, it would be *so much worse* when Zach returned and someone—twenty million someones—all of them related to him—told him that his mate once thought she was mated to his cousin. Because then he would try to kill Wade. After already trying to kill Luke. His other cousin.

She was coming between him and all his family members.

This was terrible.

"Zach's back," Isana murmured.

Lumiki froze, then looked up.

He stood by the street, just standing there, not approaching.

She quickly jumped up and raced around the fire.

Maybe if she got to him first—even as she ran, she knew she wouldn't make it because so many damn people were closer to him than she was—argh!

She dodged people left and right—maybe they hadn't seen him yet.

Leapt over a chair, kicked aside a penguin—why was there a penguin in Bryce's yard? Jumped over a flamingo wearing a Santa hat—again why? Dodged a giant polar bear —not a real one (again why?) and flung herself in Zach's arms.

He staggered back, then wrapped his arms around her. "Hey, Lumiki. Sorry I ran out like that. Just got so—lost my mind, I guess."

"I understand. Listen, I've gotta tell you something. It's not going to be easy to hear." She eased back. "I wouldn't tell you at all, but Isana went and blabbed to everybody and now you're going to hear about it and I don't want to hurt you, but it's better if you hear it from me. For a long time, because Wade saved me from some bullies at school, my fox thought he was my mate. Nothing ever happened between us, not even when we became adults, so I just thought I'd never have a mate, and then you came along and I realized I was wrong, but yeah. So that's the story."

"That's it?"

She nodded. "Yeah."

"Yeah. I've always known that."

"What?"

"Yeah, I always knew you thought that. I always knew you were wrong too."

"What? How did—are you kidding me right now?"

"Nope. Heard you and Isana talking about it. I don't know. You guys were probably eight or nine at the time. I thought you were nuts. By the time you were thirteen, I knew you were wrong. Didn't know how I knew, just knew it. Now I know it was because I knew you were mine. You've always been mine, Lumiki, my love."

"Yo, Zach," Wade called from across the yard. "Whatcha doin' with my almost-mate?"

Zach raised his eyes to Wade. "She was never your anything, Wade. She was always mine." With that, he swooped her over his arm and kissed her.

An hour later, Isana gave Lumiki the high sign so she abandoned Zach and went off to meet up with Isana.

"Are you absolutely sure about this, Lumiki?"

"I'm positive. This is going to be great for all of them, Isana."

"All right, fine."

"You have the applications, right?"

"Yes, they're all here. You can call these people and have them come and consider all the cats at your rescue center, which is a boon for you guys, and feel free to send us any Polaroids you want. We'll continue to feature them on the tables and we'll keep handing out applications at the hostess stand."

Isana smiled. "All right then. Let's do this." She turned to Mason. "Can you guys bring me Snowball to start with?"

"That's the white one, right?"

"Yep. She's the only one we're going to put in a gift bag," Isana said. "The rest are staying in their carriers."

"You got it."

"I'll be hanging with my brothers."

THE PARTY WAS WINDING DOWN AND NOW everyone was just lounging in the snow, talking.

He idly wondered where Lumiki had wandered off to.

"All right. I think it's time," Isana said. "I know you guys have been wondering who the lucky bear will be."

"What's she talking about?" Zach asked, glancing around at his brother and cousins.

Bryce shook his head, a look of surprise on his face. "Really? You didn't see this coming?"

"See what?"

"It's been a difficult decision," Isana said. "You're all worthy, so I want to assure you, I've got a gift for each of you."

"I'm lost," Wade said.

"Me too," Luke agreed.

"Me three," Steve said.

Bryce shook his head. "I wonder if it's because you're triplets."

"What are you talking about?" Wade asked.

"Just thinking maybe you each only got a third of a brain, instead of a whole one. It would surely explain a lot."

All three of his cousins let out a rumbling growl, and Bryce grinned. "Are we gonna rumble?"

"No!" Isana snapped. "Don't even think about it. I have an announcement and you lot need to be listening."

Bryce chuckled. "All right, Isana. Lay it on them."

She glared at him. "You know I could change my mind and choose you instead."

"Good luck with that. You're not manipulating me again."

Isana's gaze shifted over his shoulder. "Or I could tag your mate."

"Don't even think about it," Bryce growled at his sister.

"What's going on?" Jennifer asked as she plopped down in Bryce's lap.

"My sister's about to hand our cousins a few gifts."

"Really?"

"Yep."

"What kind of gifts?" she asked Isana.

"The very best kind."

"Oh." From the look on Jennifer's face, Zach thought she had an idea what kind of gifts Isana thought were the best kind.

For that matter, Zach had a good idea what kind of gifts Isana liked as well. Except he knew for a fact that Isana was *against* giving pets as gifts.

Although she *had* given a cat to Bryce. Zach eyed Bryce speculatively and Lumiki *was* going to try to finagle the situation so she would do the same with Zach.

Maybe Lumiki really had worked a miracle.

Apparently his cousins were having the same kind of thoughts because they suddenly scrambled to their feet.

"Oh, hey, um, I think—" Wade began.

"Yeah, we've got to—" Luke said at the same time.

"Don't even think about it," Isana said. "Sit down right now!" She waited until both Wade and Luke were seated before continuing.

"As I was saying, this was a tough choice." She looked up as Mason arrived at her side.

He gave her a nod and held his hand out.

She grabbed his hand and he pulled her to her feet, then handed her a gift bag that was clearly fairly heavy as she held it from below. "Thanks, love."

She turned back to them. "Now that Bryce has adopted Shredder, I've realized we need more pets in this family. After all, who better to take care of poor homeless animals than shifters?

"So, I've decided to start this year's gift-giving with Zach."

Zach did his best to look panicked. Actually, now that he thought about it, he *was* panicked. What if she gave him some other animal that *wasn't* Snowball? What if she gave him an animal like Shredder? "What are you talking about, Isana?"

"Merry Christmas, Zach." She stepped over to where he was sitting and leaning down, placed the gift bag in his lap.

He hesitated, almost afraid to look inside.

Finally, with a tiny growl for courage, he removed the tissue from the bag and breathed a huge sigh of relief when a tiny white head popped free.

"Congratulations, Zach," Isana said. "This cat's for you."

Zach tried not to show how relieved and happy he was as he carefully lifted Snowball from the bag and cradled her in his hands.

It was entirely too cold outside for a tiny kitten so he unzipped his jacket and settled her inside, then zipped it up so just her head was peeking out.

She lifted up and licked the underside of his chin, which made him chuckle.

Lumiki plopped down in the snow next to him and

leaned in to pet Snowball. "Told you it would work," she murmured softly.

Zach grinned at her.

Isana walked back over to Mason, picked up a carrier from the ground, checked inside, then walked over to Wade. "Wade, these cats are for you. Two gray tabbies and their mama. They need a happy home."

"Damnit, Isana."

"You can keep them at the bar. That's fine. They seem perfectly happy there."

Wade sighed. "Fine."

She smiled and walked away, only to return a few moments later to stand before Luke. "Luke, this cat's for you."

He frowned. "I'm hardly ever at the restaurant."

"I think he'd enjoy being an executive kitten at the Worcester Group since that's where you spend most of your time nowadays."

He groaned. "Isana, just because your mate loves kittens doesn't mean kittens are allowed inside the building."

"Actually it does," Mason said. "Memo's gone out already."

"Well, that's just asking for trouble," Luke muttered.

Isana skipped back to her mate, grabbed one final carrier and headed back, this time to stand in front of Steve.

"And finally, Steve, this cat's for you. She needs to live at the restaurant because that's her safe zone, okay?"

Steve stared up at Isana, a stunned look on his face.

The orange tabby inside the carrier meowed.

The moment Steve heard her meow, he looked inside and smiled, "Hello, my sweet little *Pastel de Nata*. Merry Christmas."

THE ICE BOX WAS SILENT AFTER THE HUMANS ALL left.

They had all had an adventure that day, but now they were back home and it was time to patrol the restaurant.

Snowball was on office duty.

She chased all the balls in the office, to make sure they were working properly and then jumped on all the climbing posts to see if they were high enough.

Perfect!

Then she ran all over the Bryce-man's desk, just to make sure all those papers were in proper order.

They were not, so she knocked them on the floor, just because.

She then added a few pens and some folders and a dangly cord thingy to the floor as well.

Oh, and a water bottle because it seemed the right thing to do.

She then raced out of the office and down the hallway to check on the others.

First, the kitchens.

It all looked pretty good.

A few spoons needed to be knocked to the floor and a couple bowls and that cup there, oh and that thing, too, whatever it was, plus that weird thing as well, oh and that.

Yes, that too.

A few more things there and that.

Perfect.

Yes.

On to the pastry kitchen.

Queen of Desserts was monitoring everything in there.

It was looking pretty good overall.

Nice job.

Snowball raced out of the pastry kitchen, through the larger kitchen and out into the dining room where Chef Z was currently sleeping on a bench under a table.

Hmm.

Snowball jumped up onto the table, leaned over as far as she could go and began to bat at Chef Z's dangling tail.

Hey, it was right there and it was just begging to be caught.

Whack, whack, whack.

Whack, whack, whack.

Oooh, salt shaker.

Floor.

Pepper.

Floor.

Ketchup.

Floor.

Fun.

Fun.

Fun.

Napkins.

Floor.

Snowball jumped up and leapt onto the top of the next booth, then leapt onto that table and began to bat those things onto the floor.

Salt.

Pepper.

Ketchup.

Oooh.

Pen!

She leapt down and raced across the room.

She skidded under a table and attacked a pen lying there.

It skittered across the floor.

She followed and attacked it again.

It skittered away.

Hey! Stop that!

She chased it and attacked again.

Fun, fun, fun!

She chased the pen all the way across the room until it ran right up against the bar.

Which reminded her.

It was time to check on Amaretto and Kahlua.

She hopped onto a bar stool and from there onto the bar

itself, where she found them sound asleep on a bed of mistletoe.

So predictable.

She sauntered down the bar, knocking napkins and coasters off every now and then before hopping down and exploring the backside of the bar.

So many interesting things back there.

Not to mention all the weird smells.

Still, everything seemed quite acceptable.

Time to find mama.

She always liked to hide this time of night.

Get away from the kittens, find herself a place to get high.

Hmm.

Snowball peeked into each of the cabinets under the bar.

Not that one.

Nope.

Nope.

Nope.

Aha!

And there she was.

Mellowed out from all that catnip.

Guess the twins came by it naturally.

Snowball crawled into the cabinet and curled up next to her mama.

This was the life.

The life of a good restaurant kitty.

By day, taking care of Zach-the-man.

By night, patrolling the restaurant and organizing things into their proper places.

Snowball was definitely living her very best kitty-cat life.

Read on for an excerpt from Wade's story
in SANTA KITTY.

B YGUL HAD COMPLETELY screwed up a match. It didn't happen often—after all, he *was* the top matchmaking cat at Pawsitively Purrfect Matches. (That wasn't bragging. It was just a fact.)

However, because he was so good at his job, it was even more upsetting when he actually got things wrong—and boy, had he gotten a whole lot wrong with this particular match.

Of course, Bygul had no idea at the time that he'd been given the wrong information, but that was no excuse.

He was still responsible for doing his own research and verifying all the facts, which he had clearly failed to do effectively, which made the entire situation his fault.

He took full responsibility.

This was why Bygul was determined to make things up to the polar bear he'd wronged. All that work to try and match poor Wade Meier to an arctic fox who wasn't even his mate.

Their efforts had probably gotten the polar's hopes up, only to dash them to pieces.

The bear was undoubtedly heartbroken, believing he'd been so close to having a mate, only to lose her to his own cousin.

It was shameful and Bygul was to blame.

His brother Kalyn shared some of the responsibility, of course.

In truth, Kalyn had made the situation much worse.

If Bygul had been there, he would have realized immediately that he had the wrong information and would have changed strategies immediately.

Unfortunately, Kalyn was a bit dense.

So he'd followed Bygul's instructions to the letter, stubbornly clinging to the idea that the fox was meant for Wade and not his cousin Zach.

Of course, Kalyn *was* a cat, and stubbornness did come with the territory.

Even Bygul wasn't immune. Of course, *he* used his stubbornness for the greater good.

It was why he was such a good matchmaker. Well, that and the fact that he'd been trained by the goddess, Freyja, herself, thus ensuring his place as the top matchmaker for Pawsitively Purrfect Matches.

No one had beat his record to date, and undoubtedly, no one ever would.

Because Bygul *never* gave up.

Which meant he was determined to make things right. After all, he'd committed to finding that polar bear a pawsitively purrfect match, and no matter how long it took, Bygul never failed to keep his promises.

Sometimes it took quite a while to find the right match, but this time, Bygul found her almost immediately.

She was purrfect for Wade Meier, though the polar might not agree, at least not at first.

Chances were, the woman wouldn't agree either.

It wasn't because Tessa was human. After all, she'd known about shifters ever since her father mated one when she was little.

And it wasn't because Wade was too stupid to realize she was his mate. Ultimately, he *was* a bear so that was totally expected.

No, the real reason this mating was a challenge was because Wade Meier and Tessa Madison got off on the wrong foot from minute one.

Basically, they hated each other on sight, but it was like Bygul always said: hate was only a swish of the tail away from the glory of love.

Besides, Bygul had a plan involving a number of earthbound cats and one tiny kitten in particular.

This match was going to be purrfect.

Tessa Madison should never have agreed to move in with her cousin and best friend, Keri.

Sure, she'd been in fairly dire straits at the time.

Her asshole boyfriend had cheated on her and unfortunately, their apartment lease was in his name, which meant Tessa was unexpectedly homeless right before the holidays.

Of course, Paul had been willing to let her stay, as part of the "open" relationship he felt was his due. He'd actually expressed shock that Tessa had the audacity to expect monogamy from the man she'd invited into her bed and her body.

What a *dick*.

Shouldn't monogamy be the default expectation? She'd moved in with the man, for goddess' sake. She hadn't thought she needed to explain the parameters of a respectful live-in relationship.

Obviously, if he wanted an "open" relationship, he should have informed her of this before she'd ever moved in. At the very least, they should have had a conversation about it.

According to Paul, though, Tessa was entirely too old-fashioned.

"Everyone's in open relationships now, darling," Paul had informed her. "You've been brainwashed by outdated societal expectations. Open relationships are the wave of the future. If you want to have any sort of relationship this century, you're going to have to accept that fact."

He'd then proceeded to inform her that she was welcome to stay now that she had a clearer understanding of what she could expect from their *modern* relationship.

Tessa, rage so intense she'd been afraid for them both, had simply told him she needed time to process this information and had asked him to give her the day.

He'd agreed, a rather smug look on his face, and had left to spend the day at a buddy's house, no doubt saving them both from disaster, for he'd been seconds away from dismemberment and she from imprisonment.

The moment he was gone, Tessa had called Keri, who'd shown up with half their pack, a rental truck and about a thousand collapsed boxes.

Tessa had then proceeded to take everything she'd paid for out of the apartment.

Everything.

By the time they were done, Paul's apartment was mostly empty except for his ridiculous stereo system and television that spanned the entire wall of their living room.

It wasn't her fault he'd gotten rid of his queen-sized bed when she'd moved in with her deluxe king.

Or that he'd gotten rid of his sagging sofa in favor of her leather sectional.

It wasn't her fault that he hated to cook so only had the bare minimum in supplies until Tessa had moved in with an entire kitchen full of appliances and pretty much every kitchen gadget imaginable.

It took them a while to get everything packed and loaded into the truck, which was why Tessa kept expecting Paul to show up and for there to be a massive confrontation between the local wolf pack and her asshole ex.

She wasn't certain whether she was relieved or disappointed when he never showed.

Either way, she figured it was probably for the best.

She left a note and her key to the apartment on the kitchen counter, right where her espresso machine had stood not long before.

The note had simply said, "The answer is no."

As if he wouldn't have figured that out the minute he walked into the apartment.

She'd wanted to write more, with a stream of profanities, but she'd resisted temptation.

Of course, once everything was out of the apartment, Tessa had nowhere to take it all, so she went online and rented a storage unit not far from her former apartment.

She marveled at the wonders of technology as she downloaded the storage facilities app and opened gates and her unit's garage door from her phone.

Once everything was moved into the unit, without anywhere else to go, she'd ended up following Keri back to her apartment complex, where Keri had somehow managed to convince Tessa to stay in her guest room through the holidays.

"Besides, if I make it through Thanksgiving without bailing on the family, it'll be a miracle," she'd informed Tessa.

Of course, she'd been right.

The minute Keri's mother started nagging her about finding a mate at Thanksgiving dinner, Tessa knew it was all over.

How Aunt Martha never figured out that her harping on Keri's unmated status at Thanksgiving always resulted in her daughter never being around for Christmas, Tessa had no idea.

The minute they got back to the apartment that night, Keri started packing.

"Because she's bad enough on Thanksgiving," she explained while scooping toiletries into a duffel bag, "but Christmas with my mother will drive me mad."

Tessa's response had been a simple roll of the eyes since she knew Keri would be gone for far longer than just the Christmas holiday.

"I won't be back before February," she proved Tessa right by saying next. "So you can take as long as you need to find a new place. Of course, I hope you choose to stay and we can be roommates again, or if not, that you'll move into a different apartment here."

Keri'd been trying to convince Tessa to move into her complex for years.

There was a reason Tessa had always refused though.

Tessa was thoroughly, one hundred percent, depressingly human.

Keri had never held that against her, of course, but Tessa just couldn't imagine living in a shifter-owned apartment complex in the middle of Worcester Falls, surrounded by bears and wolves and other shifters.

Sure, she'd lived with a wolf pack through much of her growing up years, but they were all family in a sense. Worcester Falls, on the other hand, was full of bears—giant, cranky, obnoxious bears—and Tessa, frankly, found them a little intimidating.

When Tessa had been in her teens, she'd had dreams of one day meeting a wolf shifter, who would instantly know she was his mate, similar to what had happened to her dad when he met her stepmom. By the time she'd graduated from college, though, she'd been pretty certain that wish was not going to come true.

As a result, she'd moved to Pleasantville, a decidedly human town, as a means of keeping herself grounded in reality. She was *human* and needed to remember that, rather than allowing herself to get caught up in fantasy dreams that had little basis in reality.

Pleasantville wasn't far from Greensboro, where the pack lived, or from Worcester Falls, where Keri had settled to get some distance from the pack, so it served Tessa well, allowing her to stay connected with the people she loved while also providing enough distance to accept what would never be.

Of course, accepting had led her to Paul the dick and her latest circumstances, living in a town she'd always avoided, in her best friend's apartment, surrounded by predators on all sides.

Keri, of course, had insisted everyone in Worcester Falls was "super-nice" and that Tessa would be perfectly safe there, but Tessa wasn't entirely sure.

Especially after meeting the polar bear who lived across the hall.

He'd hated her on sight, though Tessa had no idea why, and honestly didn't care, because it was better that way.

Better because Tessa had been instantly attracted to the rude bear whose level of hotness could not be overstated.

She hated that she'd noticed him at all and worse that she'd been so busy checking him out the first time she'd seen him, it had taken her several moments to realize he hadn't been at all interested in returning the favor.

Instead, he'd been glaring daggers at her.

Rather than feeling embarrassed that he'd caught her checking him out, she'd been annoyed.

Men had been ogling women for centuries, yet somehow this bear took offense because she'd had the audacity to do the same to him.

Just the thought of the hypocrisy annoyed her every time she remembered that moment, which was why whenever they encountered each other since, she'd taken great joy in glaring daggers right back at him.

This non-speaking, glare-filled relationship of theirs was

a little more than a month old when Christmas morning finally arrived.

WADE MEIER WAS EXHAUSTED.

The week before Christmas was always non-stop parties and endless rounds of drinks at his family's restaurant, The Ice Box.

Wade managed the bar at the restaurant, which meant he worked the later shifts and during Christmas week, those shifts went even later than usual.

This meant he was horribly cranky and groggy when someone started pounding on his door Christmas morning.

He'd think it was his bear relatives—brothers or cousins —or even the arctic foxes, but any one of them would have knocked a whole lot louder, which was saying something because whoever was at his door was determined and loud enough to make his head ache.

He tried to ignore it, but they just kept knocking.

Finally, with a roar of true frustration, he flung off his blankets, dragged on a pair of jeans and stormed toward the front door.

He flung it open and roared, "What?" in the startled face of his very human neighbor.

"Your kitten escaped," she snapped, not seeming at all intimidated by his roar.

"What are you talking about?"

"This kitten. It's cold out here. You need to be more careful."

He blinked bleary eyes at her, trying to get them to focus on the tiny form she was shoving in his face. "That's a kitten."

"I just said that. She's been sitting right here, on your doorstep, patiently waiting for you to let her inside."

He blinked some more at the kitten. She was entirely too small to be either Kahlua or Amaretto and was also the wrong color. "It's a brown tuxedo kitten."

"Huh?" She pulled the kitten back to take a look. "I mean, I guess so. Are tuxedos brown?" She waved a hand as if to dismiss the question. "No matter. The point is, it's *your* brown and white tuxedo kitten. So here."

She shoved the kitten at him again and this time, out of pure reflex, he caught the little one in his hands.

He stared down at her, charmed in spite of himself when she immediately started purring. He was so distracted, he almost missed the woman attempting to walk away. "Hey! Where do you think you're going?"

"It's Christmas morning." She whirled to glare at him. "I have better things to do than care for your misplaced, neglected kitten."

He scowled and pulled the kitten closer to his chest as if he might be able to protect her from the human's callous words. "You're in cahoots with my cousin, Zach, aren't you?"

She looked confused. "What?"

He lifted the kitten to stare at its neck. "There's no tag. What about a note?"

"Huh?"

"Was there a note? Maybe one that said, 'This cat's for you?'"

"What are you talking about? Of course, there wasn't a note."

"Well, there should be one because it's not my kitten."

"Are you sure?"

He gave her an exasperated look. "Yes, I'm quite certain this kitten does not belong to me, no matter what Zach may have told you." He glared at her suspiciously. "What about you?"

"What *about* me?" She looked shocked. "It's not *my* kitten. I don't even live here. I'm just housesitting for Keri. Besides, the kitten was on *your* doormat. Obviously it belongs to you."

"Or maybe you put it there. On purpose."

"Are you serious right now? Where would I get a kitten and *why* would I dump it on your doorstep?"

"Two words. Zach. Meier."

She shook her head. "Never heard of him."

He scowled. "Well, since you found the kitten, I guess that means *you* get to keep her." He stalked across the hall and dumped the kitten back into the woman's hands. "If you need help figuring out how to care for her, you can call Zach's sister Isana, who now that I think about it, is probably the mastermind behind all of this."

"The mastermind behind what? And I told you. I don't know who this Zach person is, so how would I know where to find his sister?"

"Yeah, right." Wade stalked back into his apartment, shutting the door behind him, but then he just stood there, actually *worried* about the kitten.

Letting out a low growl, he turned and looked through his peephole.

His neighbor was pacing up and down the hall between their two doors, a scowl on her face.

As she made a turn and paced back the way she'd just walked, he could see she was cuddling the kitten close to her chest with one arm, while waving the other and ranting.

Great.

He'd left the kitten in the care of a crazy human.

Start reading SANTA KITTY today.

Other Books by Pepper

THE MURRYSVILLE COALITION

The Crazy Cheetah Lady

One Sad Kitty

A PAWSITIVELY PURRFECT MATCH

Catnapped

The Real McCat

Unbearably Cute

A Catmas to Remember

This Cat's for You

Santa Kitty

Hocus Purrcus

Tridents & Tails

Abra-Cat-Abra

Satan's Kitty

Valen-Cats

Vampurr Lovin'

A Beautiful Cat-ship

Grave Cattitude

THE SHENANIGANS SERIES

Shifter Shenanigans

Witchy Shenanigans

Full Moon Shenanigans

Hotel Shenanigans

Dragon Shenanigans

Undercover Shenanigans

Spooky Shenanigans

Holiday Shenanigans

Valentine Shenanigans

Lucky Shenanigans

STORIES OF THE VEIL

Guardians of the Veil

Astra

Glory

Luna

Zara

WICKED

No Rest for the Wicked

Wicked Is As Wicked Does

STORIES OF THE VEIL

THE UNVEILED

Astra | Glory

THE VEILED

Luna | Zara

WICKED DUET

WICKED

No Rest for the Wicked | Wicked Is As Wicked Does

About the Author

WWW.PEPPERMCGRAW.COM

PEPPER MCGRAW is a USA Today Bestselling Author of paranormal romance. Her life to date has sadly been paranormal-free, but she knows it's simply a matter of time before her fated mate finally appears. Until that glorious day arrives, she keeps herself busy writing (and reading) paranormal romances.

Pepper loves animals, especially cats, and spends her free time volunteering at local shelters and for Trap-Neuter-Release programs. She's had the supreme honor of winning occasional head butts and meows from the local ferals in her neighborhood and has even convinced a few to come inside and adopt her as their own.

BB bookbub.com/authors/pepper-mcgraw

f facebook.com/ShenanigansSeries

g goodreads.com/peppermcgraw

instagram.com/peppermcgraw_author

tiktok.com/@peppermcgraw

twitter.com/peppermcgraw